BUZ STANFIELD - 9-1-10

Nash, Metropolitan

Nash, Metropolitan

Frank Sennett

Five Star • Waterville, Maine

First Edition
First Printing: October 2004

Published in 2004 in conjunction with Tekno Books and Ed Gorman.

Set in 11 pt. Plantin by Carleen Stearns.

Printed in the United States on permanent paper.

Library of Congress Cataloging-in-Publication Data

Sennett, Frank.
    Nash, metropolitan / Frank Sennett.—1st ed.
        p. cm.
    ISBN 1-59414-246-7 (hc : alk. paper)
    1. Journalists—Fiction.   2. Chicago (Ill.)—Fiction.
    3. Russians—Crimes against—Fiction.   4. Homeless people—
    Crimes against—Fiction.   I. Title.
    PS3619.E66N26 2004
    813′.6—dc22   2004053345

This one's for Heather,
an excellent journalist and an even better wife.

Acknowledgements

This series wouldn't be rolling along without Mary Smith at Five Star, who has been a great champion of Nash Hansen and his adventures. Mary, thanks for believing in Nash—and for putting up with me.

Thanks also to the editorial team of Ed Gorman, John Helfers, and Pat Wallace, all talented writers themselves. Speaking of which, I'm also grateful to my friend and publicist Stu Wade for getting the word out about the books.

And to M. J. Carlson—thank you for helping me get into the game in Chicago way back when. Finally, I'm sorry I can't give Dick Schwarzlose a copy of this book and settle in for a spirited conversation about the state of journalism. You were an enduring inspiration to thousands of Medill alumni, Dick, and we all miss you.

Prologue

Shortly after Kosarov transferred from the Moscow KGB to the agency's British field operation in 1987, he fell in love with the Hollywood cinema. The glitz, the glamour, the fanciful, improbable story lines—all provided a wonderful tonic to the starkly realistic style he had come to know in his homeland. He especially loved the English spy who wore tuxedos, slept with beautiful women and shot his German pistol all day without once reloading.

How he wished to live the high life like James Bond. But his expense account would not even cover the dry cleaning bill on a tuxedo, let alone a line of credit at the baccarat table.

This thirst to join a higher class had prompted Kosarov to embark upon his capitalist experiment. After raiding the files of industry and government on his infrequent trips back home, he simply sold the lucrative secrets to the highest bidders in Britain's public and private sectors. Soon he wore suits of Italian linen, drank single-malt whisky from Waterford crystal and frittered away most of his weekends in Monte Carlo.

After the coup and the rise of Yeltsin, the espionage opportunities in the new Russia grew exponentially. As the security state crumbled, Kosarov spread his hard currency around liberally. But then Putin rose to power, and sticking around began to seem like a sucker's bet. Six months later, his luggage laden with microfilm, he decided to take a shot at the big time and set up shop in the United States.

On his first day in New York City, Kosarov treated himself to a horror movie in a plush Manhattan multiplex. Munching hot popcorn with real butter and sipping a Coke, he imagined the rest of his life as a long and stellar chapter in the American success story. He would dispose of his inventory within a year and then retire to a sprawling estate in southern California with a Ferrari in the driveway and a starlet by the pool.

On screen, a man in a mask broke a young woman's neck, interrupting Kosarov's fantasy. He chuckled softly at the sound, like a thick carrot snapping in half. Even Hollywood couldn't get everything right, Kosarov thought as he tore open the seal on a box of Milk Duds. The real sound of a neck breaking was much more exciting than that.

Chapter One

"This isn't a story, Nash. You can't write it the way you want."

The sound of Elizabeth's ragged breathing coursed through the speaker, buffeting Nashua Hansen's brain. Sitting cross-legged on the living room floor of his Evanston, Illinois, two-flat, he listened silently to the end of the break-up speech. Then, resting the cold glass of Wild Turkey next to his knee on the dark blue shag carpet, he hit the rewind button on the answering machine to go over it one more time.

She had called him at 3 a.m. Thursday after working all evening on a photo shoot in Los Angeles. Elizabeth had always wanted to work with real rock stars, so she had jumped at the chance to assist her mentor, Wolfgang Prong, on a rising indie band's cover shoot for *Rolling Stone*.

That, and she wanted to take time away from a relationship at the tricky crossroads between steady sleepovers and commitment. At least that's what Nash suspected, even before she had phoned to deliver The Speech. He hit the play button and took a long pull of bourbon as her voice came on.

"I've been offered a chance to style the band's next video."

"Decorating sets for MTV," he said. "Quite a coup."

"Are you being sarcastic?"

"Not at all, honey. I'm really happy for you. Are they nice guys?"

"I'm not even sure. I just fixed the lighting and tried not to look impressed. My attitude worked, too. The manager offered me the job over dinner."

"I've never even heard of them."

"Jesus, Nash, welcome to the Millennium—they've been on top of the college charts for two months. There's more to music now than Van Morrison and the Rolling Stones, you know?"

"I heard they'll be coming out with those new eight-track tape players pretty soon, too."

"Don't be an ass."

"Sorry, Liz. So when's the shoot?"

"I'll start scouting locations and digging up props next week." She paused a significant pause. "The director's good. He could be the next McG."

Nash let that one go by without comment. It was too easy. But he did have to wonder about a culture that afforded respect to half-named idiots who went from shooting music videos to directing *Charlie's Angels* sequels.

"We ought to have film in the can in about a month," Liz continued.

"That's cutting it awfully close to vacation time."

"About that, Nash. I need to talk to you about that."

"Okay," he said, drawing out the second syllable, waiting for the other shoe.

"I'm not going on vacation with you, Nash. After the video shoot, I'm going to Grand Cayman with Wolfgang for the *Sports Illustrated* swimsuit shoot. After that, I'm not sure. But I'm not coming back to Chicago."

"You're kidding."

"No. Very serious."

12

"You sound so calm."

"I've been crying all evening about this. I guess I'm just too drained to feel any more tonight."

"What's that supposed to mean?" he asked, the first white flashes of anger breaking through his confusion. "I thought we were in love. Moving in together, vacationing in Mexico. Christ, you call out of nowhere to break up and you're too fucking drained to feel?"

"Look, I'm sorry. I just can't live with you, Nash. I don't know if we're meant to be together, and moving in with you is the same as an engagement for me. I can't take that step when I'm not sure."

"What's it going to cost?" he asked. "You know you can move out anytime you want, no strings, no questions. Don't you think you owe it to this relationship to give it a shot after we've invested two entire years?"

"Twenty-one months."

"What?"

"We've been together twenty-one months. And no, I just can't do it."

"Did you find someone?"

"I wouldn't cheat on you, Nash. Give me one iota of credit."

"But you have no problem breaking up with me."

"I don't think I can like myself and this relationship at the same time."

"Would you care to be a bit more specific?"

"I don't know if I can grow any more as a person unless I take some time out for me."

"What are you now, a radio shrink? Let's forget the psychobabble bullshit and just cut to the chase, shall we?"

"I knew you wouldn't understand."

"I wonder why I'm having trouble getting my head

around this. Let's see: It's three in the fucking morning and the woman I see and love every goddamn day of the week calls up and dumps me because I'm some kind of human caffeine, stunting her growth as a person. Now why the hell wouldn't a reasonable man be able to understand that?"

"It's time to move on."

"Right, right. Let's go over all the reasons why. Do you still love me?"

"Yes."

"Do you enjoy our time together?"

"Mostly."

"Have I ever discouraged you from following your passions? Told you to quit your job and keep house, give up Tae Kwon Do, anything like that?"

"You've always encouraged my interests."

"Well, I can definitely see now why it's time to call it quits. I'm surprised we waited this long."

"I hate it when you get sarcastic, Nash."

"And I hate it when you act like an irrational bitch."

"You have a right to be angry. This isn't your fault."

"So if I'm such a good guy, why can't we give this a chance?"

"It feels wrong to me, that's about as well as I can say it."

"You know, if I wrote this all up as a story, nobody would believe it."

"This isn't a story, Nash . . ."

He slammed his fist hard onto the stop button, cracking the machine's plastic tape cover and knocking over the bourbon as he did. Nash set the rocks glass upright and scooped three linty ice cubes into his hand. Then he just sat there a while, ice dripping onto his pant leg, crying and watching the spilled bourbon spread its sweet-smelling brown stain. After five minutes, he opened his hand to let the ice fall into the glass but found only a few rivulets of water running down his palm.

He wished he'd been fast enough to pick up the phone before the answering machine had clicked on. The conversation poked fresh holes in his heart every time he listened to it, yet he had replayed it obsessively all morning.

It was best to get moving, before total numbness set in. He busied himself for an hour cleaning the already tidy apartment in a manic frenzy as he listened to Keith Richards' *Main Offender* disc on full volume. It was only 6 a.m., but Nash's downstairs neighbor didn't complain about the noise; he worked the night shift at a White Castle on the north side of Chicago and wouldn't be home until nine or ten.

When the CD ended, Nash put away the rest of last night's dinner dishes and went into the bathroom to pee. He turned his head to take stock of himself in the full-length mirror on the door. He looked terrible. Elizabeth had installed the mirror last year when she found herself spending the night at his place three or four times a week rather than heading back to her bare-bones efficiency just up the block from Wrigley Field. Now he wanted to break the glass, but he couldn't quite work up the energy.

Nash stared at himself and wondered what had changed to make Elizabeth cut him loose. He wasn't much different physically, except that his hair was becoming a little darker every year; when he'd renewed his driver's license a few months back, the clerk had finally changed the color from blond to brown. But he was still in his mid-twenties, still five-ten, still hanging tough around one seventy-five. He zipped up and headed into the living room for some more bourbon.

What else had changed over the last two years? he wondered as he dropped Frank Black and Eels discs into the CD changer. Elizabeth was a photographer's assistant when he met her at a club opening he'd covered, and she was a photo assistant now. He had earned his journalism master's degree from Northwestern and picked up a job with the *Sentinel* metro desk, but he'd steadily freelanced stories for years. He lived in the same apartment, drove the same car, ate at the same restaurants, enjoyed the company of many of the same friends. He'd settled into a comfortable life, and until this morning he imagined that Elizabeth had come along to complete the picture. Beautiful, professional, spunky Liz.

"That bitch," he said as he dialed the city desk to tell whoever answered the phone that he was taking the rest of the week off.

At noon, as he uncapped a fresh fifth of Turkey for lunch, Nash stopped trying to figure out what had happened. After all, the relationship had probably been doomed from the start. She had been reared in a Lake Forest mansion; he had grown up in a noisy northwest side apartment building on the restless border between Korean and Latin neighborhoods. Daddy gave Elizabeth money whenever she went more than two weeks without an assignment, while Nash tried to budget payments on $20,000 in student loans out of a starting reporter's salary. He brought the bottle to his lips and took a slug large enough to make his pores vibrate.

He couldn't see how two people with such different backgrounds could make a life together. He should have called it off the moment he found out she'd never been inside a bar that didn't take credit cards. Got to pay attention to those early warning signs.

Finding the Eels suddenly too loud, Nash cut off the disc, plopped down on the couch and flipped on the TV. *Give me a working-class girl every time,* he decided as he drifted off in front of Game Show Network reruns. Chuck Woolery mocked him in his dreams.

Chapter Two

On the fourth day after the break-up, a Sunday, Nash borrowed a battered Remington ten-gauge from Slant Williams, his old Northwestern adviser. He laid the shotgun in the trunk of his rusty BMW 2002 next to a box of all the presents Elizabeth had given him, and then drove to a Cook County forest preserve twenty miles west of Evanston.

Nash pulled the car off the road at the edge of a small clearing surrounded by thick stands of spruce and pine. Emptying out the box item by item, he set up a shooting gallery. He propped the blue corduroy baseball cap on top of a fence post, the brim slanting downward so the letters of Elizabeth's college sorority were plainly visible. On the wooden fence railing he lined up the last gift she'd given him before she walked out—a set of five frosted beer mugs from Crate & Barrel. He hung the PlayStation 2 deck by its control pad wires from the lower branches of a tall spruce, then walked to the far edge of the clearing and placed the blue lava lamp on a large stump.

On his way back to pick up the shotgun, Nash glanced at his watch, wondering when the weekend jogging crowd would start huffing down the main trail. As he watched the second hand sweep past the Eddie Bauer logo underneath the six, he realized this, too, had been an Elizabeth gift. Disgusted, he undid the black canvas band—she'd often told him he could upgrade to leather if he wanted to—and soon felt the satisfying crunch of yuppie chronograph beneath his left tennis shoe.

The ten-gauge was heavy enough to make the muscles in his right arm twitch after he picked it up and dialed the choke down to the tightest shooting pattern. Nash pumped a shell into the breech, aimed at the Sony deck swinging in the light breeze, and squeezed the trigger. The Remington's kick didn't knock him over, but the force of the backlash combined with the gun's thunderous report to send him stumbling a few steps back.

Rubbing his sore right shoulder, Nash resolved to tell Slant that only a true masochist would fail to add a rubber pad to the butt of a weapon this powerful. The shot had sheared two large branches off the spruce and turned a kid-proof piece of electronics into a mass of blackened circuit boards and twisted hunks of plastic. The satisfaction he gained from creating so much carnage almost made up for the tenderness in his arm.

Nash firmed up his footing and sent several loads of steel shot toward the beer mugs and baseball cap. The opening blast disintegrated three mugs and knocked a fourth to the ground; the next shot fell low, stripping the brown paint off a large section of railing as it cut the last mug in half and sent a hunk of frosted glass flying at least ten feet in the air. With the rich scent of gunpowder liberating his nostrils, Nash aimed the third and fourth loads at the hat, spinning it off the fence post and turning it into so much corduroy cheesecloth. For the final shot, Nash dropped to one knee and took aim at the lava lamp about twenty yards away. Resting the stock of the Remington against his tingling shoulder, he took a deep breath and exhaled slowly before tugging on the trigger.

The lamp busted open like a clay piñata, sending a

shower of thick shards and white goo in a wide arc around the stump. Nash laughed loudly, reveling in the spectacle of the lava's final eruption. Whistling the theme from *The Great Escape*, he locked the shotgun back into its case and began throwing the remnants of his life with Elizabeth into a cardboard box.

As he gathered the last manageable shards, Nash found he was part of a duet. Somewhere in the clearing, a small animal had begun chittering away, and the noise was growing louder and more desperate in tone. Curious, Nash dropped the box and circled the area.

Ten feet behind the stump he found the source of the noise: An angry squirrel, covered in lava slime, was hobbling toward the forest with a large chunk of lamp-glass embedded in its back. As the squirrel admonished him for his reckless behavior, Nash felt a reservoir of self pity and anger flow from his body.

"Aw, fuck," he said to no one in particular as the squirrel slumped to the ground, wild-eyed and breathing like a child at the end of a hard cry.

After retrieving the scraps of Elizabeth's sorority hat from the box, Nash scooped up the exhausted animal and worked the glass out of its sticky fur.

"Hey now. Hey now," he told the squirrel over and over as he cradled it in the hat and placed it on the passenger seat of the 2002. As Nash drove to a veterinary hospital he knew of on Golf Road, the animal, too weak and disoriented to move, shivered violently and made half-hearted clicking noises.

Shit, shit, shit, he thought as he weaved in and out of the growing throng of afternoon shoppers cruising around the Golf-Mil Shopping Center. Elizabeth had often told him he should learn to vent his frustrations in a more mature fashion. He'd see some kid turned into a crispy critter because of a faulty space heater and then spend two hours pulverizing softballs in the batting cages on Clark Street. Or, after interviewing the family of an elderly woman beaten to death with a crowbar for twelve dollars in food stamps, he'd take the afternoon off and drive the expressways like a maniac.

Elizabeth would tell him to talk to a counselor, to buy a rowing machine, to just plain grow up, unable to understand that the intensity of his emotions gave him focus and helped make his writing sing. He could never explain the concept to her properly, mostly because she refused to listen. He slammed the dashboard with his fist and startled the squirrel into a frenzied fit of chatter.

"The hell with the both of you," Nash said. "You wouldn't know real passion if it bit you in the ass."

"I found him as I was jogging past a shooting range," Nash told the horrified receptionist as he placed the hat on the animal hospital's check-in counter.

"It looks like he's been tortured," she said.

He could see where she got the idea. The greasy lava goo had turned the squirrel's fur into a spiky, tangled mess that looked like a toupee for aging punk rockers—until it stood up and peered woozily over the side of the cap.

"I'll get Doctor Sam," the receptionist said, tossing Nash a suspicious glance as she hurried into the back room.

The procedure took forty-five minutes. As Nash looked on, a young vet in a spotless white lab coat gave the squirrel a warm bath with disinfectant soap, cleaned out the remaining glass particles with a pair of tiny tweezers and sewed up its back with four precise stitches. These she bandaged with white gauze.

"Is he a pet?" the vet asked as she washed her delicate hands in a stainless-steel utility sink mounted on the wall.

"Not quite," Nash replied. The squirrel, looking much refreshed by the bath-and-stitches treatment, chittered away in a wire cage well stocked with sunflower seeds.

"Those stitches are too far back for him to chew on, but lots of bad things happen to wounded animals in the wild," the doctor continued.

"He looks to be doing pretty well to me." When Dr. Sam smiled, he noticed she had very even white teeth.

"You're paying for the treatment anyway, so you might as well get a companion out of the bargain."

"Great," Nash said. "What time should I pick you up?"

She laughed at that one and ran a damp hand through her collar-length black hair, pulling it back to reveal one double-pierced ear.

"Him," she said, pointing at the cage. "I meant him." The squirrel was too busy gorging itself on seeds to notice the attention.

"What if he has rabies?"

"Tell you what, I'll run a full diagnostic and throw in the flea powder for free. When he's fully recovered, you can re-lease him back into the suburban wilds." Without waiting for an answer, the doctor slipped on a fresh pair of thick rubber gloves and hoisted the preoccupied squirrel out of the cage.

"I don't know what he eats besides sunflower seeds," Nash said, trying to work up a convincing protest while Dr. Sam leaned down to grab a can of bug powder from a low cabinet shelf. As she stood up and turned her attentions to her small patient once again, he thought: *If this woman ever decides to change careers, Liv Tyler will be out of a job.*

"Maybe you could tell me what squirrels eat over stuffed

pizza at Carmen's," he said.

"I can give you the full squirrel diet plan in five seconds: nuts, seeds and berries. What would we talk about then?" She turned to meet his eyes briefly, pushing the hair back again, smirking.

"Squirrel hygiene, squirrel housing, squirrel sleep habits, the whole ball of wax."

"Sounds fascinating," Dr. Sam said, capping the powder. She stroked the back of the squirrel's head with her left forefinger. "Unfortunately, I'm the only vet on duty this weekend, so I'm brown-bagging it in my office." She nodded toward a small room in back, a supply closet with a desk. "That's what happens when you're fresh out of vet school."

"You're low cat on the scratching post."

"Exactly."

"Then I'll join you for a PB&J."

"It's *pad Thai*. And I only brought enough for one."

"I think I'm being blown off here," Nash said as Dr. Sam placed a small cardboard box full of squirrel in his hands.

"You're very astute." She picked up the admittance slip and studied it briefly. "Mr. Nash Hansen of Evanston."

She made a notation on the slip and handed it to him. "Give this to the receptionist when you pay. And one more thing."

"Yes?"

"You can fix your new pal up with everything he needs at the pet supply across the street."

He knew this latest rejection should have laid him lower than ever, but as he emerged into the intense afternoon heat Nash felt somehow revitalized. Back in the chase. And Dr. Sam seemed well worth pursuing.

★ ★ ★ ★ ★

After setting up the requisite steel-mesh cage, food and exercise implements on a high end table overlooking the dying oak in his front yard, Nash poured himself two fingers of bourbon and watched the squirrel take a nap in its new home.

He sipped the Wild Turkey instead of inhaling it in one gulp, a sign that the worst of the storm had passed, at least for the moment. He focused on an image of Dr. Sam in her white coat, trying to re-create her in his mind. What did he know about her? More questions than answers. How did she keep that coat so clean dealing with animals all the time? Did her hair smell like dog at the end of the day? Was she from the city or the suburbs? And, most importantly, would she ever give him a chance?

Basta! he thought, remembering one of the most useful Spanish words his friend Curt Escobar had taught him down in San Bernardino. *Enough!* Nash put a vintage John Lee Hooker disc on low and stood at the window. Sloshing the last of the drink around in the tumbler, he tried to come up with a name for his new pet.

Rocky, as in Bullwinkle's buddy. *Most lame,* Nash thought, rocking back and forth to the insistent pulse of Hooker's gravelly voice. He turned to survey the coffee table and noticed the remains of Elizabeth's sorority cap on the floor next to it. Three Greek letters, now shredded and drooping onto the bill, had proclaimed her affiliation to the Michigan State chapter of Tri Delta Epsilon.

He had carried the squirrel to Dr. Sam's clinic in that hat. The image gave Nash an idea. He tried to remember all the names he knew from Greek mythology, but none of them seemed to fit the gently heaving ball of fur resting at the bottom of the cage. Finally, he settled on a fellow writer: Thucydides, the historian who chronicled the Peloponnesian Wars between Athens and Sparta around 430 B.C.

He put his face up against the cage and whispered, "Hey, Cyd." Although the squirrel kept its eyes closed, Nash thought he saw its tiny ears twitch in what might have been a sign of recognition.

"Hey, buddy, hope you enjoy that big wheel I bought you," he said, a little bit louder now. At that, Cyd's eyes popped open. The squirrel sat up on its haunches and cursed Nash out with a barrage of chittering before settling back down for some more sack time.

"I know how you feel," Nash said, heading off to the bedroom to catch a few hours of sleep himself.

Chapter Three

The newsroom of the *Chicago Daily Sentinel* looked the same as it had when Nash left it on Thursday afternoon; except for the computer monitors blinking away on every desk and the fluorescent lighting panels spaced evenly across the expanse of off-white ceiling, it hadn't seen major changes in at least thirty years. He felt comfortable in these rumpled surroundings, filing stories by six every evening for the early edition of the city's third-largest—and scrappiest—newspaper. Instead of the cubicles he'd briefly known at the *San Bernardino Ledger*, ancient partner desks remained beautifully exposed here in the *Sentinel's* smoky nerve center. Nash shared a scarred mahogany unit with thirty-year-old Jerry Povaric, the resident mass transit specialist and his best friend at the paper. When Nash sat down at 9:45 Monday morning, he found Jerry pitched forward in his ergonomic knee-rest chair, tapping out a piece on fare-card fraud at the Chicago Transit Authority.

"Glad to see you again, Mr. Hansen," Povaric said, tilting back slightly on the bizarre seat so that his small belly curved the pinstripes of his silk shirt. Although he was of average height, Povaric's long limbs made him look somewhat gangly, an impression enhanced by his awkward pose. "How's Lizzie?" he asked.

"We shall now refer to her as Elizabeth Dade Pulliam," Nash intoned.

26

Povaric's blond eyebrows went up so that the creases on his forehead scrunched into long speed bumps of flesh. "You serious?"

"Very serious."

After Povaric's second wife had left him a year earlier, he and Nash decided over several pitchers of beer that all women who rudely dumped their men—or men who blew off their women, for that matter—should thereafter be known by their full names, like assassins and serial killers. Reporters had included the middle name of John F. Kennedy's assassin in their stories to keep the innocent Lee Oswalds of the world out of trouble. The same rule had applied to John Lennon's killer, Mark David Chapman, and hundreds of lesser-known scumbags who made the papers as a result of their murderous natures over the years. And if it was good policy for killers, Nash and Povaric figured, it was good policy for dirty lowdown heartbreakers as well.

"God, Nash, I'm sorry." Povaric's look of surprise softened into a sympathetic frown. "I thought you two were a permanent item. And now it's Elizabeth Dade Pulliam? Forever?"

"I think so. But the good news is, I met a possible replacement over the weekend."

"You remind me of a shark—move forward or die, right? So what's her story?"

"She's an animal doctor from River North. Dr. Sam. Think Liv Tyler."

"Wow. Does she have an older sister?"

"I'll ask—if I can get her to go out with me."

Povaric's eyebrow shot up again at that one. "How about a middle name?"

"I hope not," Nash said.

Povaric laughed and turned his computer screen toward

Nash. "Could you give this crap the once-over before I turn it in?"

"Sure. This the one about sticky fingers down at the CTA?"

"Yep. Finally got the official response this morning. They're going to install new cameras at all manned El stops to cut down on theft."

"Why don't they just hire honest employees?"

"The way the old system worked, when the folks behind the glass were cashiers instead of customer service reps, you'd have to be an idiot or a saint not to take advantage of the scam possibilities. But the temptation was supposed to go away with the fare-card system."

"Machines don't cheat."

"Right," Povaric said, leaning forward to save his document. "Unfortunately, some of these booth jockeys with too much time on their hands found out how to pop the machines, skim the fives, tens and twenties, then lock 'em back up with no one the wiser."

"Especially with supervisory staffs cut to the bone and the CTA cops riding the rails to bust the pickpockets and shell game cons. It's great stuff, Jerry. How'd you catch it?"

"Disgruntled ex-employee, shitcanned for lighting up a joint on his break. So he calls me all pissed off because he's on the street while everyone else in his section keeps defrauding the system for hundreds of dollars a month. Dumb prick thought I could get his job back. First a doper and now a whistle blower—you think the CTA is looking for that kind of headache?"

Nash shook his head. "Did anyone miss me while I was gone?"

"Shit, those were the first sick days you've taken since you started here. You're entitled."

"Benton didn't say anything?"

"Nah. It was a slow couple of days what with the Sporting Goods Show moving out."

Nash had been working the trade show beat for the past six months, a pretty good assignment considering that Chicago boasted the largest exhibit hall in the United States: McCormick Place, two point two million square feet of steel, glass and concrete perched on the banks of Lake Michigan just south of Soldier Field, Shedd Aquarium and the Field Museum of Natural History. It hosted the usual mix of boat and auto shows, along with huge trade fairs for the nation's major manufacturing and service industries.

He covered the economic impact of the shows, new product unveilings, business trends and any major crimes that turned up. Occasionally Bea Benton, the business editor, would give him a specific assignment, tell him to profile an important convention speaker or look into reports of trouble with the Teamsters. But Nash came up with enough of his own angles to file twenty inches a day and a major feature at least once a month. Stories about the biggest shows and the most exciting products often landed on the front page, but most of his pieces ended up buried in the business section. It wasn't bad work, but it was definitely a dues-paying beat.

Nash made his way over to Bea Benton's corner desk, tapped her left shoulder and said, "Hey chief." At that, the business editor dropped her *Wall Street Journal* onto a massive pile of folders, papers and assorted junk, then swiveled around on her squeaky chair and coughed.

"Mr. Hansen. Welcome back to the land of the living," Benton said. Her eyes watered from too much smoke, too little sleep and too many hours at the computer screen.

"I'm glad you noticed I was gone. Povaric said things ran

29

fine without me, which always makes me nervous."

"Welcome to the machine, my friend. We're all just bricks in the wall."

"You know, Bea, if you weren't my boss, I'd have to tell you quoting Pink Floyd lyrics went out the window with the last acid freak who thought he could fly."

"That's the problem with you Rolling Stones fanatics— it's not rock 'n' roll if you can understand the words."

"Tune it in, turn it on and rip the knob off."

"Speaking of which, I wanted to talk with you about covering the National Electronics Exhibition."

"Move-in was this week."

"Right. The show opens tomorrow, and they're letting the public in for the first time ever. Management wants to get the consumers all hot and bothered over the new big-screen TVs while the exhibitors write their retail orders for the year."

"And you want me to find out what Joe and Mary Sixpack think of all the fancy gimcracks and gewgaws."

"That'll be one story, yes. But I also want you to take the readers through every step of the trade show process, from set-up to teardown. Give me a different angle every day. How does the convention bureau book a show into town? What goes into setting up one of those video wall exhibits? What types of retailers come to the show? What's the hottest product segment? How far away are the electronics junkies going to come from for the first public day? I'll assign someone else to do all the new products stuff to free you up a bit."

"Sounds good. I'll have the first piece on your screen tomorrow morning."

"How about late this afternoon? I'm getting pressure from on high to feed the Web edition, too."

"I was afraid you were going to say that."

"Run like hell, Nash."

"See you on the dark side of the moon, Bea."

"Now you're getting it," Benton said. As Nash walked away, the business editor turned back to her stock quotes and began whistling the chorus of "Comfortably Numb." Thank God there were still a few human beings left in the business worth working for.

Chapter Four

If McCormick Place could be considered a city unto itself, with all its restaurants, business centers, security battalions, and resident homeless population, then Gil Francis was mayor for life. The president of the Windy City Convention Bureau, Francis had been holed up in the subterranean depths of the massive complex for longer than anyone could remember. But it wasn't longevity alone that gave him the substantial clout he enjoyed in both city politics and the nation's trade-show industry. Francis possessed the two traits most revered by Chicago power brokers: a genial personality and intimate knowledge of where all the bodies were buried.

Nash found the fifty-six-year-old Francis hiding out in his Spartan office tucked neatly into the southeast corner of the bureau's windowless headquarters. He was hard at work climbing a Stairmaster while he flossed his teeth, one-handed, at the same time. If it hadn't been for the Botox injections, his forehead might have wrinkled from the effort.

"The working press arrives," Francis said out of the side of his mouth as he worked the floss between two tough back molars. "Care to join the workout?" He gestured to the high-tech stationary bicycle resting beneath a picture of Wrigley Field on the eve of its first scheduled night game, a rainout on 8/8/88.

"Why the hell not?" Nash said, shedding his sport coat

and setting the timer for a mile and a half.

"I'm up to five miles a day on that bike," Francis said as he dismounted the climbing machine just long enough to discard the gooey string of floss into a nearby wastebasket. "I do it all before nine a.m., when I'm making calls to the East Coast. Thank God for speaker phones."

Nash, pedaling hard and already feeling somewhat winded, nodded in agreement.

"I bet you're here to cover the electronics show. And you need me to run over the highlights for you, the inside dish."

Nash nodded again. He lifted his feet up for a moment as he pulled the micro-cassette recorder out of his shirt pocket and hit record. His background sessions with Francis always went like this. They'd either work out in the office or take a long constitutional around the grounds while Francis dished up intricate details of the local business scene, sometimes for attribution, sometimes not, but always right on the money. Francis briefed him so thoroughly in these meetings that Nash rarely had to ask a question. That and the fact that the exercise put an end to the small beer belly Nash had developed a few months back made the bureau president a pristine source.

"Juan Masters flew in from the electronics association's headquarters in New York last week to renegotiate the show's long-term contract with us. He asked for all sorts of concessions, work-rule changes so he wouldn't have to use so many union crews, cuts in the hotel rates. The man was asking for the impossible, you know?" Francis took a long swig from the water bottle hanging on the Stairmaster's handlebars.

"I smelled a rat, so I asked him if he was under pressure to bring the show in cheap. Masters tells me the exhibitors don't see the need for a winter electronics show in Atlanta and a summer session here. Most of the deals are done in January, so the buyers use the June show mostly for window-shopping. Basically, letting the public in is a last-ditch attempt to save the summer expo. And Masters wanted to hedge his bets by getting some extra long-term breaks for his exhibitors.

"The bottom line, Nash, is that Chicago stands to lose one of its most profitable shows if things don't go really well this week. We're talking tens of millions in direct economic impact every year."

Nash lifted his feet again and watched the bike's pedals slow to a halt. "And that's where I come in?"

Francis stepped off the climbing machine, patted his forehead with a clean white hand towel, and clicked off Nash's tape recorder.

"Look, Nash, I've given you lots of good tips the past six months, right? Six or seven front-page stories."

"And I've appreciated every one of them," Nash said. "So drop the other shoe already."

"Okay. I'm not asking you to make up facts or anything, I want you to understand that. All I want is for you to play up the positives a little more than your instincts might tell you to."

"For instance?"

"For instance. Pre-show ticket sales to the public have not been as high as we had hoped. The hall might not look as full this week as you'd expect after two million dollars in regional hype. I'm calling in my chips to ask you to over-look droopy attendance figures, disgruntled exhibitors, buyers who don't like sharing space with the *hoi polloi*."

"Gil, all my editor wants from me this week is happy talk anyway. Your request is duly noted." Nash wondered how many other local media types Francis had put the touch on

34

in the past week to make sure the spin on the show coverage came out exactly right.

"I thank you, the city thanks you, and the Teamsters would thank you, except they're on a break at the moment." Francis shook Nash's hand and signaled for his secretary to come in. The meeting ended as abruptly as it had begun.

After spending an hour schmoozing the convention bureau's sales staff to get a handle on the booking procedures for a major trade show, Nash took the escalator up to the main level of the east building of McCormick Place. Now known as the Lakeside Center, it was the oldest of the three exhibit halls on the campus. Watching workers assemble 30,000-square-foot exhibits with cranes and giant forklifts, he felt like an extra in a Godzilla flick.

When the exhibit hall sat empty, it looked like an abandoned aircraft hangar, only bigger. But in the space of two or three days almost every week, the facility's labor force pulled off a magical transformation, turning the space into a vibrant marketplace with wall-to-wall carpeting and enough lighted displays to make the folks at Caesar's Palace green with envy.

Nash made his way past swearing carpenters and electricians, around a mountain of orange, purple and green indoor-outdoor carpet, and through a plywood frame that would soon look like a personal computer on growth hormones. Overwhelmed by so much disarray, he made his way to the phone bank in the hall's registration area and called Dr. Sam at the pet hospital.

"Squirrel problems?" she asked when the receptionist he'd offended grudgingly patched him through.

"Just squirrely." He thought he heard half a giggle on

the other end of the line.

"Look," Dr. Sam said. "This is an especially busy time of day for me."

"Then I'll make this especially quick: As odd as this sounds, I'm a reporter at the *Sentinel* and . . ."

"That doesn't sound so odd."

"The odd part is, when I told my editor about Cyd . . ."

"Cyd?"

"That's what I named our furry friend."

"Hmmm. I like it."

"Thanks. Anyway, when I told my boss about him, it gave him the idea to run a piece on offbeat pets. And guess who got the assignment?"

"I don't know if I like where this is headed."

"Strictly business, I swear," Nash said. He crossed his fingers. "I'd like to pick your brain on the subject, maybe over lunch tomorrow?"

"Can't tomorrow. Nash, there must be several hundred veterinarians you could talk to within the city limits . . ."

"But I don't know any of them," he said, sensing this was his last shot. "It's always harder to interview somebody you've just met, and that's assuming I can find someone willing to talk before my deadline. Besides, I figure a suburban vet would have more experience with off-the-wall pets than a city vet. Your clientele has more money, more living space . . ."

"All right, all right," Dr. Sam said. "But tomorrow's still too hectic."

"How about tonight? Dinner. Your choice of restaurants. It'll be fun."

"I don't know . . ."

"Come on, give a working stiff a break. I rarely get a chance to put dinner on my expense account."

Long pause. Nash could hear a dog yowling in the background. "Well, since you put it that way, I'll go," she said. "If you can meet me outside my office by six-thirty."

"Done. By the way, do you go by anything besides Dr. Sam?"

"Samantha Parker, but Sam's just fine."

Chapter Five

In just over six hours, Nash would be picking up Samantha Parker at the Golf-Mil Veterinary Clinic. His first-date skills were hopelessly rusty. Maybe Sam would play Dorothy to his Tin Man and make everything okay; she seemed like the type who didn't mind taking charge. Maybe that's what he needed, to let someone else take control of his next relationship, guide it to a place where they'd both stay happy.

Stepping off the elevator into the newsroom, Nash banished thoughts of Samantha from his mind. From the way everyone was running around like ants sprayed with gasoline, he knew something big had happened. After three near-collisions with scurrying staffers, he made it to his desk and looked around for a familiar face to give him the scoop. Instead, he spied a familiar back—Bea Benton's—on its way to the main conference room. As the door swung open, Nash could see the room was full to bursting with reporters and editors from every section. *Always room for one more,* he thought as he jogged once again across the floor.

"Good. We're going to need you on this one," Benton whispered as Nash slid in next to her against the back wall.

"Who got shot?" Nash asked.

"I wish it were that small," Benton said. "Two jets got into a head-on over O'Hare about ten minutes ago. Early word: no survivors. Casualties in the hundreds."

"Holy shit."

"Yeah."

"Terrorism?"

"Hasn't been ruled out, but it would take some pretty fancy flying to run into another jet. Besides, terrorists would go for Sears Tower over a measly airplane. Best guess is a missed signal in an overcrowded sky. But TV and radio are getting the citizenry into a panic."

Similar conversations going on throughout the room raised the noise level to airport runway levels—until Phil Silvestri, the young metro editor Nash dealt with whenever his stories made it out of the business section, hopped onto the long conference table and bellowed for silence.

"Enough with the rumors," he shouted. "Here's the news: At twelve-seventeen p.m., two 737s—a National and an Air Colombia—collided over O'Hare. Observers reported a bright orange fireball visible for twelve miles. No survivors have been found. Wreckage fell on several runways and at least one nearby neighborhood. All flights into O'Hare have been re-routed to regional airports and all outgoing flights have been canceled indefinitely. No passenger lists yet, but there were as many as two hundred fifty people on board the jets. First reports indicate the Colombian plane was taking off and the National jet was coming in when the collision occurred. And that's all we know.

"Right now, the editor and managing editor are in conference upstairs and we're priming for constant Web updates on this one. And that means everyone drop what you're doing and pick an angle. We're also going to need volunteers on the rewrite desk—I want all our field reporters to phone in what they've got as soon as they get it.

Now, I need info from all section editors: How many writers do you have available, what angles do you have in mind, and how much space can you give me?"

The meeting, a model of wartime efficiency, wrapped up in fifteen minutes. Writers and editors streamed out of the room with a focus and singleness of purpose that made Nash's spine tingle. They were going to wrestle this story to the ground from literally dozens of angles, including but not limited to: the political response from Washington and Bogota; how many VIPs were on board; reactions from families of victims; the crash's effect on the stock market; a history of plane crashes in Chicago, the nation and the world; any discernible causes from the FAA; an overall evaluation of safety at O'Hare and, for good measure, Midway airports; biographies of the pilots and crews; a search for anyone who was supposed to be on board but missed the flight or decided not to go; even a travel piece on what to do in case of several types of airline disasters.

To get the Web extras rolling, most of those stories would have to be told in some form by 3 p.m. And Silvestri had pegged Nash to go into the affected neighborhood and interview bystanders. Three hours to make some sense out of the situation. He had no time to think; movement was key.

On the way to grab fresh tapes for his recorder, Nash almost knocked over Povaric, who appeared to be in a similarly frenzied state.

"Those bastards have all taken their phones off the hook," he shouted as he slammed his receiver home. "I've been trying every source I have at the airport for twenty minutes. Nothing."

"Why don't you drag your ass out of the chair and head out there?" Nash asked.

"I don't have a car."

"Oh yeah, that's right. Sorry. For a second there I thought I was talking to the goddamn transit reporter."

"Fuck you."

"No, fuck you. And come on, I'll drop you off on my way to the wreckage."

They made good time out of the garage and onto the expressway, but, with two lanes under construction, traffic on the northbound Kennedy was crawling.

"Unbefuckinglievable," Nash yelled as he inched along behind a late model El Dorado with plates that read "Gas Hog."

"There's nothing we can do about the wait," Povaric said. "We might as well try to relax."

"And here I forgot to bring my Monopoly set," Nash snapped.

A long silence ensued as he tried to make some headway by weaving his ancient BMW in and out of the three open lanes. He briefly contemplated riding the shoulder, but knew he'd never get all the way back across the expressway in time to catch the left-hand split to O'Hare.

"You know who I like?" Povaric asked suddenly.

Nash took a deep breath and resigned himself to his fate. "That new copy editor with the honey-brown tan?" he guessed.

"Well, yeah. But I mean celebrity-wise."

"Who?"

"Jennifer Jason Leigh."

"Yeah?"

"I just rented *Miami Blues* the other night," Povaric continued, "with Alec Baldwin."

"You were watching videos with Alec Baldwin?"

"He stars in the movie, shithead."

"Just checking."

"Anyway, it's a thriller from the eighties. Jennifer Jason Leigh plays this young hooker named Pepper, right? And she fucking *nails* that certain knowing naiveté, if that makes any sense."

"Like she seems all sweet and innocent but she really knows the score?" Nash asked. They were close to where the Kennedy peeled off from the Edens and traffic was loosening up. He cut hard into the far-left lane.

"Not quite," Povaric said as Nash gunned the motor in second gear and slid between a double-trailer rig and a giant SUV. "See, she *is* sweet and innocent, but she's got the wisdom to know right from wrong combined with the strength of a survivor."

"Plus she's cute."

"Goes without saying. Absolutely gorgeous."

"Is she naked?"

"Why do you have to bring it down to that level, Nash?"

"Is she?"

Povaric grinned. "Oh yeah."

They merged into the O'Hare traffic, which soon became thin enough to allow third-gear driving. They did not yet see any smoke on the horizon. "It seems like most of the really hot actresses these days have three names, you know?" Povaric said.

"What about Liv Tyler?"

"Jesus, what's with the Liv Tyler fixation?"

"Nothing. I'm just poking holes in your theory is all."

"Oh yeah?" Povaric said. "I bet I can come up with more three-name babes than you can of the two-name variety."

"That's a sucker bet," Nash said. "You're on."

"You start—and Liv Fucking Tyler does not count."

Nash paused, trying to think of a good one. "Charlize Theron."

"Sarah Jessica Parker," Povaric shot back.

"Cameron Diaz."

"Sarah Michelle Gellar."

"Jennifer Garner."

"Mary Louise Parker."

"Bridget Fonda."

"Um, Mary Tyler Moore."

"That's kind of a stretch, isn't it?" Nash said.

Povaric shook his head. "Picture those Capri pants she always wore on 'The Dick Van Dyke Show.' "

"True enough."

"Your turn," Povaric said.

"I'm thinking. Okay, here's one. A classic, an all-time great: Myrna Loy."

"Shit yes," Povaric said, thumping the dash. "Nora Charles from the Thin Man movies. Smart, saucy and an absolute knockout."

"So I win?"

"Not quite. Melissa Joan Hart."

"Sabrina the Teenage Witch!" Nash said. "She still seems like jailbait to me."

"I'd say Chris Evert Lloyd then, but she doesn't go by that name anymore. Besides, she's in the booth these days. I guess I'll have to give up," Povaric said.

"But since you brought up the wonderful world of women's tennis, might I mention Anna Kournikova?"

"Ah, Anna K." Povaric took a deep breath. "I love the way she grunts."

"I love the way she sweats."

"Thighs of iron."

"And a terrific overhead shot."

"A pretty good ball-handler all the way around."

"That's what she said."

"That's what who said?" Povaric asked.

"Haven't you heard that before? You can turn almost any sentence into a suggestive phrase by adding, 'That's what she said.' We used to do it all the time at North-western."

Povaric snapped his fingers. "That's my problem. I didn't go to a candy-ass journalism school to learn what a lead is."

"Oh yeah, I forgot. You're the tough guy who clawed his way up through the late, great City News Bureau."

"Damn straight. The best education a journalist could ask for. While you wrote up mock obituaries from phony fact sheets, I was checking out real stiffs at County."

"Gee, Uncle Jerry, why do you even hang out with a guy like me?"

"Missionary work," Povaric said.

As they came to Cumberland Road, Nash spotted plumes of black smoke rising from a row of houses a few miles east of the airport. He exited into the O'Hare traffic loop and dropped Povaric off at Arrivals.

"Bet my call beats yours to the rewrite desk," the transit reporter said as he hopped out.

"Don't count on it," Nash said. But Povaric had already run halfway to the terminal. The dashboard clock read 1:25. He had an hour and a half to find the story and phone it in.

"Nothing but time," he said as he drove toward the smoke.

At 2:48, Nash pulled into the parking lot of a 7-Eleven and punched the paper's switchboard number into his cell phone. Thirty seconds later, he had the rewrite desk.

"How're we coming?" he asked. The anonymous staffer on the other end of the line would soon be feeding his raw copy into the computer and forwarding it to the copy desk for a quick once-over, a headline, and then up onto the Web. With everyone working at top capacity, the story's trip from mouth to cyberspace might be as short as twenty minutes.

"We'd be fine if we weren't trying to pull together tomorrow's print edition at the same time," the voice said.

"You ready?"

"Shoot."

"Graph. Stanley Wheat—W-H-E-A-T—has grown accustomed to the constant din of airplanes taking off and landing at O'Hare airport, a scant two miles west of his home of thirty-nine years. Period. But he was unprepared to come home for lunch Monday and find the tail section of a National 737 jet embedded in his roof. Period.

"New Graph. Wheat was one of dozens of residents of this usually tranquil neighborhood whose homes were pelted—Dash—and in six cases destroyed—Dash—by flaming debris from the cataclysmic mid-air collision of two jets at twelve-seventeen p.m. Period. . . ."

By 2:58, Nash had transmitted fifteen inches of copy on the destruction, including illuminating quotes from Stanley Wheat and several firefighters and cops at the scene. He was riding an incredible deadline high.

"By the way," the rewrite man said as Nash prepared to hang up. "Jerry Povaric phoned his story in about half an hour ago. He said you'd want to know."

"Thanks," Nash said, shaking his head. "Thanks a lot."

"Glad to help," the voice replied. "And Silvestri says to tell everybody in the field we need new leads and additional reporting on your stories by six for tomorrow's editions."

So much for enjoying the triumphant glow of a job well done. Nash thanked the man once more and pocketed the cell. *Thank heaven for 7-Eleven,* he thought as he walked into the air-conditioned comfort of the convenience store. This had definitely turned into a Super Big Gulp kind of day.

Chapter Six

After doubling the length of his original story and tacking on a new lead, Nash made another call to the rewrite desk at 5:30. Ten minutes later, he swung the 2002 east for his appointment with Sam. He hoped the adrenaline buzz would last a few more hours.

A block from the clinic, Nash took stock of himself in the rearview. Not a pretty sight. Nor, for that matter, a pleasant smell. After a moment's deliberation, he decided he had just enough time to high-tail it to his apartment for a change of clothes. But when he walked in the door, the VCR flashed 6:15. The clock had finally beaten him.

"Just fucking great," he said, skidding into the bathroom for deodorant, toothpaste and a quick swipe of comb through his matted hair.

He stripped down to his underwear on the way to the bedroom and, once there, threw on a clean black Mickey Mouse T-shirt, gray ragg wool sweater, and pleated brown chinos. Two mismatched socks and a pair of topsiders later, Nash roared due west on Golf Road in the moderate Monday night traffic. As the dashboard clock clicked ever closer to 6:30, Nash shifted into fourth and pressed the 2002's narrow gas pedal to the floor. He felt more alive right now than he had in months. He tuned his new stereo to WXRT in time to hear the beginning of Van Morrison's "Astral Weeks."

Making exceptionally good time, Nash arrived at the clinic's parking lot by 6:43, just as Samantha Parker pulled onto Golf Road in her silver Saturn hatchback. He honked, but she kept going, heading west two blocks to Milwaukee Avenue, where she hung a quick left and began cruising south, toward the city. He continued his pursuit, running the light at Golf and Milwaukee, then pulled beside her in the left lane a few blocks later.

Nash honked again. This time she looked, then smiled, thank God. Sam waved and pointed down the road. He eased in behind the Saturn and soon found out he wasn't the only one who enjoyed driving fast. Within five minutes, they were inside the City of Chicago, where Milwaukee Avenue changes from a strip mall paradise to a closely bunched collection of ethnic storefronts. In the middle of an old Polish neighborhood, Sam parked in front of a restaurant with an unpronounceable name full of consonants and a big red apple on its sign.

"Fancy meeting you here," she said as he emerged from the BMW two spaces back. She nodded toward the restaurant. "Best smorgasbord in town. Under ten bucks a pop, all you can eat."

Monday was not a slow night at the Red Apple, Nash thought as they settled into a small corner table jammed between two boisterous parties of twelve. It was probably this busy every night; Chicago's Polish population was still bigger than any city outside of Warsaw.

They ordered iced vodka from Kamil, their native-speaking waiter, then joined the buffet line that snaked from the back of the room almost to the cash register just inside the door. As Nash filled Samantha in on the crash coverage, a continuous stream of young girls shuttled between the kitchen and the smorgasbord, bringing out stacks of clean plates and steam trays overflowing with hot food. The room shimmered with delicious aromas.

"Why haven't I ever heard about this place?" Nash asked as he floated forward in line.

"Stick with me, kid," Samantha said. "There's a lot more to life than PB&J."

While he quizzed her on the finer points of raising marmosets, iguanas, and bobcats, Nash gorged himself on pirogue, fresh fruit, potato pancakes, gooey crepes and chunks of meat so tender and greasy they slid off the bone.

The waiter brought them a pint of Stoli in a bucket of ice. "A riddle for you?" he asked.

"Why not?" Samantha replied as Nash filled two tall shot glasses.

"What is only word that changes meaning and pronunciation when you capitalize it?" Kamil said in heavily accented English.

Samatha laughed and shook her head. Turning to Nash, she said, "You're the wordsmith around here."

"Don't look at me." He downed his shot and moved to pour another one. "You're the one who wanted a riddle."

"I will give one clue," the waiter said. He leaned forward and rubbed a washcloth on the table, then stood back and pointed at himself.

Nash shrugged. "No idea."

Samatha tasted her vodka, savoring the burn. "All right, Kamil, I guess we give up."

"Is too simple—polish and Polish." They all had a good smile over that one, and Nash made a mental note to bump up the tip.

By the time they decided there was no room for dessert, they had polished off the frigid vodka.

"So you're a newspaper reporter," Samantha said, sipping at a steaming cup of coffee. "Why not TV?"

"My parents have asked me that question many times. I guess I just think there are better ways to tell a story than reading an oversimplified analysis over thirty seconds of MTV quick cuts."

"Too bad." She looked at him with mock seriousness. "You have a face America could trust."

"How so?"

"I don't know." She laughed. "Your eyes, I guess. Those long blond lashes, the intelligent stare. You actually seem interested in what I'm saying."

"It's my job."

"Gee, thanks."

"And, you happen to be quite an interesting woman. I always thought you had to travel to new places for adventure. I mean, I love Chicago, but it's always been home. All the same haunts: Cubs Park, shot and a beer at the Billy Goat, blues at Buddy Guy's, stuffed pizza at Carmen's. You grew up here, too, but you find new angles on the city every day."

Samantha's face flushed. "I'm just a glutton for new experiences, I guess."

"In my experience, that's the best kind of person to hang out with. Will you take me under your wing?"

"Are you sure you can handle it?"

"I'm willing to try."

She sized him up for several beats, regaining her poise. "Well, I have been in the market for a new sidekick for a while," she said. "You might fit the bill."

After deciding to keep the evening going, they caravanned south down Lincoln Avenue to Samantha's favorite second-run movie house and caught the final feature. Her beeper squealed during the third reel, but a quick call took care of whatever pet emergency had come up. At the end of the film, when they both stayed in their seats to watch all the credits, Sam grinned at him. Walking back to the cars, Nash took her hand and asked her to go out with him again at her earliest possible convenience.

"I'll call you this week," she said.

"I've got a better idea."

She frowned, as if thinking she'd misjudged him. "Not so fast," she said.

He held up his hands, palms out. "That's not what I meant. I was only going to ask if I could take you someplace fresh and exciting in the next few days."

"I thought that was my job. You're the creature of habit who never goes anywhere new."

"This is different," Nash said. "It's job-related. The National Electronics Exhibition opens tomorrow and I thought you might want to wander around and check out the latest stereos and movie machines."

She nodded slowly. "All that Yuppie porn makes my mouth water."

"Great, so what day is good?"

"How about tomorrow?"

"Wait a minute," he said. "This morning you told me you were booked solid on Tuesday."

"Nah, it's my day off." She smiled mischievously. "I was just trying to blow you off again. Before you won me over with your boyish persistence."

"Thank goodness for that."

"Yes. Thank goodness."

"Then I'll pick you up at your place, say about eleven?"

"Throw in lunch and you've got yourself a deal."

"Says the doctor to the poor reporter."

"Hell, Nash, even you can afford a hot dog with everything at the Weiner's Circle."

"If you're lucky, I might even throw in an order of cheese fries."

"See you tomorrow, big spender." She jotted her address down on a prescription sheet and handed it to him. Just as Nash was about to turn away, she pulled his head down and kissed him. It didn't last long, but the insistent pressure of her lips conveyed something that felt like passion.

Then she hopped into the Saturn and headed east, leaving Nash feeling better than he had any right to four days after a major break-up. It was the cheapest date Nash had been on since high school, and, as it turned out, one of the most memorable. He imagined he would even enjoy a trip to the dentist if Samantha sat in the next chair. He couldn't wait to tell Elizabeth about her.

Chapter Seven

It looked like their second date might also be their last.

"I can't believe you don't wear your seatbelt when you're going sixty miles an hour down Lake Shore Drive," Samantha said as they neared the McCormick Place exit.

"I only put it on when a song I don't like comes on the radio."

"Why's that?"

"I'd hate to die with something like 'Afternoon Delight' ringing in my ears."

"And I'd hate to see you looking like the guys in the crash photos they used to show us in medical school before I decided animals deserved medical attention more than dumb humans like you."

Nash started to buckle his shoulder harness, but then let the strap snap back into place next to the seat.

"You almost got me," he said, giving Samantha a sardonic smile as he eased the 2002 into the underground parking lot.

"I'm just trying to show you I care."

"No, you're trying to inflict your lifestyle on me. Next you'll be feeding me light beer and bringing bottles of canola oil over to my apartment. I'll die of boredom inside of six months." He dropped his right hand onto Samantha's knee to show her he was making a lighthearted attempt to set a few ground rules. But by the way she brushed his hand off her leg while staring straight ahead at a group of Japanese exhibitors returning from a late lunch, Nash knew he had stumbled into trouble.

She glared at him now, smoldering, ready to blow. "I don't think now is exactly the time to start extrapolating our relationship six months into the future. If I were you, I wouldn't bank on us being together the next six minutes. I can't stand it when guys are too pigheaded to accept a friendly piece of advice."

This was the time to apologize. He knew that much, but for some reason he didn't feel like backing down. Maybe he was projecting his anger at Elizabeth onto Sam. Maybe he was just too damn stubborn for his own good.

"So now I'm 'guys,' " he said. "Since you've decided to lump me together with every man you've ever met, I'm going to let you in on one of my gender's little secrets. When we want somebody's advice, we ask for it. Otherwise, you can assume we're doing fine." He pulled hard on the parking brake.

They stared at each other for a long moment, hands on their respective door handles, trying to keep the hot flame of indignity lit. Suddenly, Samantha's grimace dissolved into a smirk. Soon, she started laughing. Nash ran his fingers through his hair, feeling stupid. And then he found himself laughing, too.

"Isn't this the part where we fall into each other's arms for a round of incredibly passionate sex?" she asked, wiping tears from her eyes.

He nodded and grinned. "I'd settle for a kiss."

"Okay." Samantha leaned toward him, but her forward motion was stopped by the shoulder belt.

"Don't you say a word," she said, giggling and falling

back against the seat. He scooted closer and positioned his face in front of hers.

"Give it another try."

She moved her head forward so that their lips were almost touching. "Why do I always fall for such independent guys?"

"Maybe you scare all the meek ones away." He tried to kiss her, but she bit his lower lip and held it between her teeth for an excruciating second.

"Smile when you say that," Samantha said as he ran his tongue gingerly over the bite mark. "Now let's take a look at this exposition. Maybe you can buy me a new stereo by way of apology."

As they walked back to the parking garage after the show closed at six, Nash decided he had been acronymed to death. In just over two hours, they had been subjected to displays for all sorts of CDs, PCs, DVDs, MP3s and HDTVs. He felt the need to catch some Zs. Even though Samantha carried half the press releases and cheap premiums they collected, he felt sure the load of crap in his arms would soon pull him to his knees.

"What's going on up there?" Sam asked, nodding toward the far end of the deserted lot. Three security guards stood in a semi-circle next to a van with flashing blue lights on top. A figure lay motionless on the ground in front of them, but the guards didn't seem to be in a hurry to do anything about it.

"Take a break here for a minute," Nash said. "This may be a story." When he turned around to set his bag on the wide concrete railing, he saw Gil Francis jogging toward him down the walkway.

"Oh, shit," Francis said when he saw Nash. "Why do

these things always have to happen when there's a reporter around?"

"What things?" Nash asked as he followed the convention bureau chief to the ambulance.

"We've had an incident," Francis said.

"Is that him lying there on the floor?"

"Shit oh shit oh shit. Nash, you are definitely a fly in my ointment today."

When they reached the scene, Nash noticed that the head security guard, a usually easygoing man named Jace, looked like he'd recently received a peanut butter enema.

"It's one a them homeless guys, sir," Jace said. He pointed at the figure lying face down in a pool of dark liquid.

"Please tell me he died of exposure or something," Francis said.

"Exposure to an ice pick maybe," the guard said. Judging by their reactions, his crew thought that was about the funniest gag they'd ever heard.

"Jace, goddamnit," Francis yelled. "Just tell me what happened."

"From the looks a things, we've got an honest-to-Christ stabbing on our hands."

Nash stepped in for a closer look. "Any idea who did it?"

"Come over here a minute," Francis said, motioning for Nash to follow him to the other side of the van.

"Now look, the last thing I need this week is 'Murder at McCormick Place' splashed all over the front page. If we don't do real good box office with the public, Chicago will flat lose this show."

"I'm sorry to hear that, Gil."

"What the hell is that supposed to mean?"

"Let's take a calm look at this situation for a minute,

okay? A man has been killed in your parking garage. The police have to be involved, and the coroner. Reports will be filed, statements will be made. Even if I didn't write this up, it would still make the evening news. As a favor to you, I'll downplay the sensational aspects as much as possible, but that's all I can do."

"I need more than that, Nash."

"My hands are tied, Gil."

"I don't think you understand what's going to happen here in the next twenty minutes. Three trusted employees of this facility are going to move this transient back into the maintenance room he's apparently been calling home and then they are going to lock the door. When the electronics show is over, one of them will 'discover' the body and report it to the proper authorities. Everybody goes home happy."

"Except him." Nash pointed at the corpse. The pool of blood had grown since they'd arrived. The man hadn't been dead long.

"Who's going to miss him? He's homeless. It's probably better that he stepped out of the room when he did."

"Maybe so, Gil. But don't you think the police should have the best possible shot at catching the scumbag who knifed him?"

"If I've got to choose between losing this city millions of dollars a year and giving the cops a slightly better chance at finding a guy who's probably halfway to Milwaukee by now . . . I'm telling you, in my mind it's not much of a choice."

"I'm really sorry to hear that, Gil."

"Don't do this, Nash. You owe me."

"It's nothing personal. But if I've got to choose between maybe helping to solve a murder and engaging in some kind of half-assed cover-up that's bound to blow up in our faces, well, in my mind it's not much of a choice."

"I can have you held."

"For a week? Come on, Gil. If you don't want me to write this story, you're going to have to fucking kill me. You know that and I know that. But we also know you're not going to kill me. We're friends. You're acting crazy right now, but I'd like to think our friendship will continue after this blows over. So let's just end this before we step over the line for good."

"I'm warning you, Nash. You run the story and you're through in this city. Your name will vanish from the address books of every newsmaker in the state. When I'm finished throwing my weight around, you won't be able to land an interview with the street sweeper at the Lincoln Park Zoo."

"Do you want to call the police or should I?"

"Fuck you," Francis whispered. "Get out of my building before I have you arrested for trespassing."

"Your mistake," Nash said.

After dropping Samantha off with a kiss and a promise to return before midnight, Nash had no problem talking to several city officials above the level of Lincoln Park Zoo street sweeper. Gil apparently hadn't succeeded in black-balling him yet. By eight, he had reported the story about as fully as he could without missing the first-edition deadline.

The facts were sketchy but predictable. Police could not yet release the name of the deceased, ostensibly because they wanted to notify next-of-kin before the story hit the papers, but more probably because they still had no idea who the guy was. What they did know was this: The victim was a Caucasian male, mid-forties, six-two, one hundred and eighty-nine pounds; blood tests showed trace levels of alcohol and no illicit substances; time of death was pegged between 5 and 6 p.m. He and perhaps one other person had lived in the storage room for at least a week. The murder weapon, a blade at least six inches long, had pierced the man's heart and left lung, but the knife had not been found at the scene. No witnesses had come forward and there were no suspects.

Privately, the public information officer at the department told Nash the detectives figured another homeless person, probably the victim's roommate, had stabbed the man during some kind of dispute. Because there were minimal signs of struggle at the scene, the officer said, whoever killed him must either have known him or surprised the hell out of him. The chances of catching the guy, especially if he was a vagrant, seemed bleak.

The story, all seven inches of it, was slated to run on page one of the Metro section. And that would likely be the end of it. Unless the killer became remorseful enough to turn himself in or the cops identified the victim as some missing socialite who'd dropped out of society, the case would hit the cold file faster than you could say coffee break. There was very little community pressure to follow up on crimes committed by the homeless against the homeless. If people thought about it at all, they probably imagined, like Gil Francis, that the man was better off dead than spending his days breathing exhaust fumes and making the passersby uneasy.

Hell, they were probably right, Nash thought as he slugged the piece BUMKILL and messaged it into the city editor's computer. It didn't take many stories like this one to turn a crusading reporter into just another cynical member of the hopeless masses. He wished the cops would actually put in the effort to solve this one; he needed a reminder that every once in a while justice was too blind to use the social register when deciding which citizens deserved a fair shake.

Maneuvering the BMW around the orange cones clogging the streets adjacent to the Magnificent Mile reminded Nash that Chicago enjoyed only two seasons—winter and construction. It took him fifteen minutes to find an empty parking space within three blocks of Samantha's loft in the River North gallery district off of Orleans Street. It took him twenty-five more to get two take-out orders of linguine carbonara from Club Lago. By the time he crossed the threshold into Sam's apartment for the first time, he felt too tired to eat.

But there she was in a thick white terry robe, curled up on the couch with a pint of Ben & Jerry's Fudge Brownie in her hand and an extremely warm smile on her lips.

"Just dump the food in the fridge," Samantha said, pointing her spoon toward the small kitchen area to his left. "I think we need to work up a little appetite before dinner."

He didn't know if it was because they'd fought earlier in the day or if it was just that they were both eager to erase the image of death from their minds, but whatever the reason, their first time together was both incredible and passionate. So was their second.

The sex started out timid, perhaps because they had known each other less than a week. The small gold hoop hanging from Sam's outie belly-button and the diamond-studded earring that pierced her left nipple surprised him. But when she assured him the ornaments caused her no pain three years after insertion, he admitted they made her seem more exotic, and that they turned him on.

These discoveries shattered a few of the preconceived notions he had about her personality—and about himself—

even after she told him the rings were the last remnants of her bohemian college days, when she briefly shared quarters with an avant-garde sculptor. Nash decided not to ask the sculptor's sex; there were a few illusions he wished to maintain for the evening.

At about four in the morning, after a fine feast of cold linguine, Diet Coke, and ice cream, they attempted to hit for the cycle. When they finally made it into the shower two hours later, Nash felt glad they had decided to press their luck.

"So, when do I get to see your place?" Samantha asked as he began gently massaging shampoo into her fine dark hair.

"I don't know," he replied, leaning down to kiss her damp shoulders. "When do I get to see yours?"

She laughed and turned to face him, the water flowing fast between them.

"Not for a while yet, I think," Samantha said as she moved in closer and began working wonders on him with the washcloth in her right hand. When he kissed her, he noticed that she tasted a bit like soap. As the tip of her tongue entered his mouth and sent a low-voltage surge of electricity straight into his brain, however, Nash realized the taste didn't really bother him at all.

Chapter Eight

Although he was sorely tempted to call in sick when 9:30 rolled around and he found himself still wearing Samantha's bathrobe, Nash sucked it up and rolled into the newsroom at the stroke of 10. Reading the memo in his mail file inviting him to an 11 a.m. meeting with the publisher, managing editor, metro editor and his immediate supervisor, Bea Benton, he congratulated himself on having the wisdom not to play hooky again after only two days back on his beat.

Jerry Povaric read the memo over Nash's shoulder and whistled softly. "What the hell did you do, buddy—fake a Pulitzer Prize–winning story?"

"You think I'm in some kind of trouble?" Nash pushed back in his chair so he could see the expression on his friend's face.

"Let me put it this way: I've never seen anybody come out of a meeting with so many swinging dicks before without a few bruises."

"I bet it's that goddamn Gil Francis."

"Jeez, Nash, I thought you two were tight as ticks."

"Me, too. He threatened to yank my chain yesterday if I filed a piece on the stiff in the parking garage, but I figured he'd cool down once he put things into proper perspective."

"Guess he thought a corpse would be bad for business at the old electronics show." Povaric shook his head. "If this story poisoned the well with a guy like Gil Francis, you're effectively through with the business beat. He can put a chill on most of corporate Chicago during one of his morning workouts."

"So I've been told."

"Good luck, buddy. You've been building up lots of credibility and good will around here since day one. If you tell it straight, I bet the brass comes down on your side. Maybe you'll even end up with a better beat when this thing shakes out."

"Thanks, Jerry. I'll buy you lunch after the meeting and fill you in."

"Are you sure you don't want to go home and change your clothes first?" Povaric grinned and gave him a fist tap on the shoulder.

"Just for that, I'm going to tell everyone at the meeting you're craving a transfer to the Home section."

"Most guys I know are in a good mood after they get laid, Nash. What's your excuse?"

"How does the Health & Fitness beat sound?"

"Okay, okay. I take it all back. Look, let's go for gyros about two or three. I'm due up at the airport to cover a killing."

"Not you, too."

"Yeah, since this guy was offed on one of those little trains that shuttles passengers between terminals, the story falls under my jurisdiction. Metro desk figures I've got better sources at O'Hare than the cops-and-crime reporters do. I guess you and I are the Duo of Death this week."

"In about forty-five minutes," Nash said, "I just might be one of your stories."

The executive conference room on the thirtieth floor of

the *Sentinel* building commanded an impressive view of Lake Michigan and the Navy Pier cultural center and expo hall. Sometimes, when Nash and Povaric worked late on a slow night, they'd sneak up here, pull two of the plush swivel chairs away from the long oak table and cap off the evening in front of the huge picture window with a bottle of bourbon and some good Sixties rock 'n' roll on the built-in sound system.

They jokingly called the room Falcon's Lair, but as Nash walked in to find a phalanx of pink-faced execs in matching pinstripes looking at him over the tops of their collective wire-rimmed glasses, he realized the name was more apt than he'd imagined.

"Mr. Hansen, thanks for coming in on such short notice." That was Avery Graf, publisher of the *Sentinel*. It was widely rumored that Graf, one of the most influential power brokers in the state Democratic Party, would soon be joining the governor's cabinet, perhaps as Secretary of Transportation. Nash couldn't tell if Graf's smile was sincere, but he didn't appear hostile. A good sign, or simply the mark of a good politician?

"Go ahead and sit down," Bea Benton said, gesturing toward the empty seat closest to the door. The business editor didn't look too alarmed by the proceedings either, but Nash wasn't ready to let his guard down yet. He took a seat and nodded a greeting to Phil Silvestri. To the metro chief's left sat Reg Devonshire, the managing editor. Devonshire was so straight-laced he argued against publishing live-model lingerie ads from Sears and Marshall Field's. Nash was mildly surprised not to see Gil Francis sitting at the table with them.

"We've convened this meeting to discuss options for covering the McCormick Place killing, and, since you were our man on the scene, we wanted to get your input," Silvestri said. He sounded downright friendly.

"If this is about that business with Gil Francis, I'd like the chance to explain," Nash began.

"What business with Francis?" Devonshire asked, leaning forward in his seat and looking to Graf for an explanation.

"Don't worry about that bullshit," Benton said. The business editor placed a firm hand on Nash's left arm.

"Exactly what 'bullshit' are we talking about?" Devonshire demanded. He spat out Benton's salty phrase as if it was a mouthful of sour milk.

"We're getting off point here, guys," Silvestri said, but Devonshire and Benton didn't look quite ready to call a truce. Nash had heard tales of bad blood between them caused by some editorial decisions Benton saw as half-assed attempts at censorship rather than solid news judgment, but he hadn't realized the animosity bubbled this close to the surface.

"Can we just finish laying out the assignment?" Benton asked. "Some of us work for a living."

"I'd like to remind you that I am your superior," Devonshire squeaked, looking to Graf for some backup.

Benton flashed a tight-lipped smile. "No, Reggie, what you are is my supervisor. And if you'd like to . . ."

"That's enough. Both of you." Although he spoke in almost gentle tones, whenever Avery Graf opened his mouth he commanded the level of respect normally accorded to drill sergeants and heads of state. It wasn't just that he was the boss; this average-looking, forty-eight-year-old newspaperman exuded a quiet charisma that made most everyone he met hope they could be his friend—even reporters trained to distrust the business side of the paper that publishers represented.

As Graf surveyed the room, a hush fell over the proceedings and both Devonshire and Benton eased back into their chairs. Finally, Graf looked at Nash and began to speak.

"Mr. Hansen. Nash. Can I call you Nash?" he asked, rubbing his smooth chin with the back of his left hand.

"By all means."

"Then I'd be pleased if you'd call me Avery. I don't think there's any place in a newspaper for standing on formality." He shot a quick glance at Devonshire before continuing. "And I also don't think there's any place in the profession of journalism for editors to hang good reporters out to dry on the say-so of an outsider—even when that outsider happens to be one of the most influential men in the city."

"I'm glad to hear that, Avery." The name sounded good rolling off Nash's tongue.

"Your piece on the plane crash was fine work. I've also done some checking on your background, Nash. For such a young man, you've published several excellent in-depth reports. I understand you had some trouble with a paper down in San Bernardino taking the word of an investigation target over yours. A man you eventually sent to prison, if I'm not mistaken."

"He should be eligible for parole in about ten years," Nash said.

Silvestri and Benton both laughed at that one. Even Graf chuckled a little. Devonshire looked bored.

"Well, we trust you Nash. You've got the *Sentinel*'s full support."

"Thank you, sir."

"Avery."

"Thank you, Avery."

Benton leaned toward Nash. "Unfortunately, we can't work miracles. If Gil Francis smears you all over town, it will hobble your work for the business section."

"Which was one of the factors in our decision to put you on another assignment," Silvestri said.

"That's right, Nash," Graf continued. "We're going to put your considerable investigative skills to work. You're about due for a promotion anyway. How does special projects sound?"

"Sounds good to me," Nash said. In fact, he felt incredibly relieved. "But I have a hard time believing you'd call me in here just to give me a new beat."

"Right," Graf said. "Let's get down to business. Do you remember a few months back when the police arrested a high school student for killing a homeless man on Lower Wacker Drive?"

"Didn't he shoot the poor guy with an arrow?"

"That's the one. When I read our account, I was absolutely sickened. That boy, sixteen or seventeen years old, went beneath the streets of Chicago and killed a man just to see what it would feel like. He brought his buddies down to the site on several occasions to show off the body. The police apprehended him only after one of the young men told his girlfriend about it and she called nine-one-one."

"Sick stuff," Nash agreed.

"The sickest. After we ran the story, I vowed this newspaper would not treat the next murder of a homeless person as a one-day story to be buried and forgotten in the metro section. And your stabbing victim is that man. As far as the *Sentinel* is concerned, the McCormick Place murder is as big as the Lindbergh baby kidnapping. Our goal is two-fold: We want to find this man's killer and at the same time remind our readers that every human life is sacred.

You will spearhead that effort."

It was some speech, Nash had to give him that. He actually felt inspired. That left only one thing to say.

"I'm already on it."

"Good, Nash. Because so am I. I'm spending some of my political capital around town to get the highest levels of the police department interested in breaking this case. You should have good access to the principal investigators throughout."

"And when they catch the guy that did it," Silvestri said, "we're going to make his trial front-page news, and you're going to handle the coverage."

"I'll miss you, Nash," Benton said. "Promise me you'll write."

"Oh he'll write," Devonshire said with a smirk. "I'll make sure Mr. Hansen writes his little heart out."

"As you may have already surmised," Graf said, "Reg will be coordinating the coverage. But don't hesitate to pick up the phone if there's anything I can do to help move the story forward." This time, he gave Devonshire a significant look. Nash hoped the managing editor understood the implicit threat: Don't fuck this up with your petty power games. He wished all the newspaper guys like Devonshire would go back where they belonged—managing the produce sections of grocery stores.

"By this time tomorrow, I want you to pick another reporter to help with the legwork," Graf said. "Just make sure it's somebody Phil can part with for a few weeks."

"We'll map out the coverage over lunch tomorrow," Silvestri said.

"Maybe we should bring Devonshire along with us," Nash said.

"Why?"

"Since you're giving me this promotion, it's only reasonable that we talk about my raise."

Before Devonshire could sputter a protest, Graf raised a hand and smiled. "Nash is right. It is a smart man who understands his own value. I'm sure you and Reg can work out the particulars. If not, well, you know my extension. It's been a pleasure, gentlemen. Now let's get out there and kick some ass."

As he boarded the elevator to the newsroom, Nash could see Devonshire was still blushing from Graf's last comment.

Chapter Nine

Billy Goat's Tavern enjoyed a hallowed place in the pantheon of Chicago attractions. Even though a discerning eye could spot two or three tourist groups cluttering the place up at any given moment, it remained one of the few honest-to-God classic bars in the city. Getting there, a difficult process that was one of the Goat's many charms, meant plunging into the city's underground street system and meandering around until one found oneself a few blocks north of the Chicago River and just a little bit east of Michigan Avenue.

Owned by the colorful Sianis family and immortalized by columnist Mike Royko at three different papers over four different decades, Billy Goat's had the unique advantage of being in the basement of Tribune Tower, and only a few blocks from both the *Sun-Times* and the *Daily Sentinel*. In other words, the Goat was an underground haven where reporters met between deadlines, drank Schlitz on tap, ate wonderfully greasy steak-and-egg sandwiches, and engaged in their two favorite hobbies—spreading rumors and telling lies. It had been Nash's favorite hangout since the day he'd made his first fake ID. His friendship with Jerry Povaric was sealed when he found out the tavern was the transit reporter's number-one haunt as well.

"We probably sat right next to each other a couple dozen times before you started at the *Sentinel*," Povaric said as he loosened his thin green tie and began working on a double "cheeboiger," as the Greek counterman called it.

"Nothing's changed since then," Nash said between bites of his ketchup-smeared rib-eye-and-fried-egg sandwich. "Except now that we know each other you've got to feel guilty about never buying me a drink."

"I'll drink to that," Povaric said, signaling the bartender for another Schlitz Dark by shaking his empty mug over the top of his head.

"Knock that off, you," the bartender hollered from the far end of the dark wood bar. "I'll get you when I'm good and ready." Povaric swiveled around on his stool and laughed. Four o'clock and the place was a tomb.

"I'd hate to see that guy deal with happy hour," he said.

"I heard that," the bartender yelled over his shoulder. He stood watching the early evening news on the ancient TV sitting above the rows of open liquor bottles. "From now on, you pay double."

Nash washed down the last chewy bite of kaiser roll with the rest of his beer. He always tried to finish his drink and his food at the same time. To him, it represented the culinary equivalent of a simultaneous orgasm. "Ah, now that hits the spot."

"Jeez, kick a guy when he's down, why don't you?"

"Sorry, Jerry. Into every life a little shit must fall. Speaking of which, what's the deal on the corpse at O'Hare?"

"I can't quite figure it," Povaric said, popping a pickle round into his mouth. "Guy in a suit, out at the airport with no luggage but a ticket to Los Angeles in his pocket, gets stabbed on the shuttle train between terminals."

"That doesn't sound so weird. Whoever killed him must have taken his luggage. That's probably why the creep did it."

"I don't think so. Guy's still got his wallet on him. I'm talking stuffed with cash."

"Okay, so somebody catches the killer in the act, he panics and runs." Nash paused to sip the fresh beer the bartender placed in front of him. "Or . . ."

"Yeah? Or what?" Povaric smacked his lips in anticipation as he watched his beer coming out of the tap.

"Or, think about this: What if the guy's in a real hurry?"

"Which guy?"

"The guy who gets stabbed. Which guy do you think I'm talking about? Try to keep up with me on this one, Jerry."

"Precision in everything, Nash." Povaric lifted the glass to his lips and inhaled two-thirds of his beer.

"So the guy's in a hurry, right?"

"You already said that." Povaric could barely get the words out around the carbonation in his esophagus.

"If you'd shut up for a minute, maybe I wouldn't keep losing my train of thought. So this guy . . ."

"He's in a hurry."

Nash threw a peanut shell at Povaric, who retaliated with his last pickle slice.

Even though he was again facing the television, the bartender yelled, "You guys knock it off back there."

"How'd he do that?" Nash asked. Povaric laughed so hard a thin stream of beer began trickling out of his nose.

"Ow," he said, wiping the beer away with the back of his hand. "I hate when that happens. Worse than a fucking ice-cream headache."

"You think we can get serious here for a minute?" Nash asked, trying, without much success, to control his own laughter.

"I don't know. Can we?"

"Just shut up a minute and let me lay this thing out. The

guy, the victim, the dead man on the train, he's in a big hurry. Such a hurry he doesn't even have time to pack his briefcase, for chrissakes. He just stuffs a big wad of bills in his wallet, figures he'll buy whatever he needs when he gets where he's going, right?"

"Could happen."

"So, what are some of the reasons a man would be in that much of a hurry to get out of town?"

"Family emergency."

"That's one," Nash said, letting loose a small belch.

"What's that, reason two?" Povaric asked.

"No. Reason two—now see how you like this one—the man's in a hurry because somebody's after him. He's running away from danger."

"But he doesn't run quite fast enough."

"Right. So, Jerry, if I may be so bold as to suggest, you find out what kind of trouble this man was in, you've got yourself a killer."

"Maybe you can help me out on that one, Nash."

"Why me?"

"Well, for starters, the cops say this guy, the victim, he's an exhibitor at the National Electronics Exhibition."

"No shit?"

"Would I pull your leg?"

"Jerry, there's two days left in the show. Management gets real pissed if an exhibitor leaves early. This guy must've been desperate to get out of town. Did you get his name, name of his company?"

"Cops wouldn't release it yet. They said they had to wait . . ."

"Until they've notified next of kin."

"Indeed."

"They get this killing on tape?"

"There's a security camera on the train, but apparently some 'bangers spray-painted it a couple days ago. Bottom line: They weren't recording when the guy was stabbed."

"Witnesses?"

"I talked to half a dozen gapers standing around while the coroner loaded the meat wagon. A few of them were waiting for the shuttle when it pulled up with the body in it. Two people told me they saw a bum shuffle off into the sunset, but neither of them bothered to get a good look at him because they didn't know there'd been a murder until they got into the car and saw the blood. Nobody ever looks too close at those homeless guys anyway."

"Do you like the transient for this?" Nash asked. "Doesn't seem quite right to me."

"Well, he was the only other person on the train when it pulled in, but maybe the killer got off between stations somehow and this poor jamoke was just sleeping in the corner or something."

"Because you'd think if a homeless guy did it, he'd take the money."

"Unless he's one of the walking wounded mental cases they let out of the state hospital whenever the funding dries up."

"Yeah, maybe. But even a crazy man has to eat."

"You know, Nash, that's so profound I just might have to write it down on my cocktail napkin."

"Everybody's a philosopher after a couple of beers at Billy Goat's."

"There he goes again, ladies and gentlemen. Profound, profound, profound."

"The first thing we ought to do is talk to the electronics show staff and find out which exhibitors left early and why."

"No way."

"What do you mean no way?"

"The first thing we're going to do is have another beer, and then we're going to have another one. After that, we'll improvise. But we're not going to haul ass over to McCormick Place right before rush hour. I've already written the first-day story on this thing; the rest of it will keep until morning."

"Jerry Povaric, I like your style," Nash said, raising his glass in agreement.

He pulled up to the curb in front of his apartment just in time to wave to his neighbor as he left for the night shift at White Castle. Nash was glad to be back home where he could use his own toothbrush and listen to his own music. Still and all, if Samantha called and invited him downtown for another night of frolicking, he knew he'd jump right back into his car.

It was immediately clear that Thucydides wasn't adjusting well to his new digs. When Nash turned on the living room light, Cyd let loose with the squirrel version of the riot act. He had tipped over the bowl of sunflower seeds, scattering them all over the floor in front of the cage, and it didn't look like he had used his exercise wheel. Nash gave him some more food and water, along with a quick pat on the head, and decided he would release the animal as soon as its injury healed.

Nash turned on the tail end of Letterman and sank down onto the couch to read his mail. A cheesy computer printout promised "Mr. Nishua Hansen" a pre-approved "Ultra Gold Card" from Finance International, Inc. All Nishua had to do to get the card was send the fifty-dollar annual fee to a post-office box in Muncie, Indiana. He decided to pass.

The only other letter he received, a chatty note from his mother and father written on pastel stationery, updated Nash on the joys of retired life in Pensacola, Florida. In the year since they'd moved into their little Gulf Coast condo, his folks had become integral members of the local seniors community, organizing polka nights, bowling leagues, fish fries and the like. They seemed determined to re-create the best aspects of the life they had left behind in Chicago. Nash wished them luck. Now that his vacation plans with Elizabeth had disintegrated, maybe he would go down and see them in a few months. He might even bring Samantha along; if she could survive a week in the land of the senile, she could handle anything.

The flashing light of the answering machine caught Nash's eye when he got up to take a leak. Thinking Sam might need a little break from his voice, he had resisted the urge to call her earlier in the evening. But as he crossed his fingers and hit the play button, Nash hoped she had called to tell him otherwise.

"Hey, pal," she began, "do you know who this is? You'd better. It's ten o'clock and I'm sad here without you. I hope that doesn't scare you. I just had to call and tell you, last night was amazing. I didn't realize what I've been missing the last few months. I'm not trying to rush things, or maybe I am. I don't know.

"Nash, I want you to know, I think we're starting in on something really good here. I can't remember ever feeling like this before. Anyway, this is beginning to sound awfully schoolgirlish, but I miss you. Call me if you get in before midnight, but don't call any later because I'm still exhausted from last night and I've got to be at the hospital by eight. Say hi to Cyd for me. Good night, lover."

Nash smiled. He moved to push the erase button but

then thought better of it. He pulled the cassette out of the machine and dropped it into the drawer of the telephone table. As he unwrapped a fresh tape, he thought: *This one is a definite keeper.*

Chapter Ten

For almost the first time in memory, Nash was showered, dressed and on the streets by 7 a.m. He hoped to get an early jump on the investigation, but first he wanted to start Samantha's morning off right with a dozen red roses and a romantic card on the doorstep of the animal clinic.

Because the only "florist" open that early was a twenty-four hour supermarket on Chicago Avenue, Nash had to settle for a rather wilted bunch of long-stems. But as he signed the card in the hospital parking lot at 7:45, he felt confident Sam would overlook this minor defect. He left the package in front of the door and hurried back toward Evanston lest she spot him on her way in. After a brief detour through a McDonald's drive-up, he arrived at the *Sentinel* by 9:00.

"I never thought I'd see you in here an hour early," Reg Devonshire said when he spotted Nash walking into the half-deserted newsroom.

"Are we still on for lunch?" Nash gave Devonshire a cheery smile.

"Twelve sharp," the managing editor said. "We'll meet at the Drake."

"Wow. It's lucky I wore a tie today."

"Yes. How fortunate."

"By the way, Reg, I'll be bringing along Jerry Povaric. He's going to help me with the investigation."

"Well, then," Devonshire said as he turned toward his office, "this really ought to be a hoot."

Povaric rolled into the newsroom a few minutes past 10, just as Nash finished a preliminary outline of the investigation. It included phone numbers of sources, the key questions they would need to answer, and various hunches and lines of attack.

"You ready to help me find the transient who killed my guy at O'Hare?" Povaric asked.

"Only if you're ready to help me find the guy who killed my transient," Nash replied.

"Hey, you put chocolate in my peanut butter!" Povaric yelled.

"You put peanut butter on my chocolate!"

"Nash, we'd better stop this nonsense. It's making me hungry."

"That's good. Devonshire's taking us to the Drake for lunch—*at noon sharp.*"

"Then let's get cracking and see what we can dig up at the electronics show," Povaric said. "If we're late getting to the restaurant, old Reg will probably make us skip the fruit cup."

"I'm sorry, sir, you'll need a pass," the receptionist told Jerry Povaric when he tried to enter the electronics show press room. Luckily, Nash had received his credentials in the mail well before his run-in with Gil Francis. Unfortunately, it didn't look like Jerry was going to be able to sneak in behind him.

"Can he still get a badge at the registration desk?" Nash asked.

"Only if he has valid media credentials."

Povaric grabbed the morning edition of the *Sentinel* off the young woman's desk and pointed at his byline above the front-page story on fare-card fraud at the CTA.

"Is that valid enough for you?"

"Come on, Jerry, she's just doing her job." Nash read the young woman's name tag and smiled down at her. "Mary, can my friend borrow your paper for a minute?"

"I guess so."

"Thanks. You've been a big help." Nash showed Mary his laminated pass as he stepped over the threshold into the press room. "Jerry, go out to the lobby and get a set of credentials. I'll try to find a flack we can talk to."

The newspaper reporters covering the show were used to fairly regular hours and Nash saw a few of them already heating up the press room's temporary phone lines, talking to editors on the East Coast or lining up interviews with exhibitors. But the magazine writers, many of them freelancers, were another story altogether.

Nash spotted three trade mag reporters and a CNN camerawoman scarfing down free doughnuts and coffee in the corner hospitality area, but the representatives of the major consumer magazines were nowhere to be found. Hotel maids around the world dreaded the arrival of freelance writers like no other guests. They rarely emerged from their rooms before noon, and even if they did, they almost always left behind mounds of junk food wrappers, discarded paper and empty booze bottles.

Nash had learned early on that the media relations staffers of most major expositions enjoyed partying with the freelancers; the only difference was, the flacks had to show up for work on time. Thus, the best time to catch a PR rep with her guard down was bright and early. After about noon, they became their professional selves once again, but at any time before lunch, they were easy to pump for information.

After grabbing one of the last butterhorns off the snack tray, Nash poked his head into Judy Harrison's office. A pleasant woman in her late forties, she was the show's highest ranking press officer, and Nash had spoken with her on the phone a few weeks earlier.

"Nash Hansen," Harrison said before he even had a chance to stick out his hand. "How did that piece on the cell phone industry turn out?"

He could gauge the skill level of any flack by how quickly they could read his name tag and remember if they'd ever met before. Judy Harrison was highly skilled indeed. Nash realized he'd have to be straight with her if he wanted to come away with any useful leads.

"Good to finally meet you in person, Judy," he said as she stood to shake his hand.

"It's a pleasure. Please, have a seat."

"I bet you really enjoy these few hours of down time in the mornings," he said as he pulled a folding chair up close to her desk.

"God yes." Harrison smiled. "If you guys worked all the time I'd have a nervous breakdown by the middle of the week. What can I do for you?"

"I need some information about an exhibitor."

"I'm afraid you're in the wrong place for that, Nash. Besides the stack of press releases in the other room, the only info we have on the exhibitors is where they're located. Have you been to this company's booth?"

"Actually, that's not possible."

"Why not?"

"The exhibitor I want to find out about was murdered yesterday."

Judy Harrison gave a surprised laugh, but when Nash didn't join her, she coughed and pushed her thick brown glasses to the back of her nose. "You're serious."

"Yes."

"What happened?"

He told her the story, what he knew of it, and asked if she could give him a list of exhibitors who had left the show early.

"I don't know if I should do that," Harrison said. "Our show manager, John Blakely, will be in the office this afternoon. I think I should talk to him first."

"I understand you're nervous about this Judy, but I really need the information. If I have to, I can wander around the floor until I find an empty space and ask the exhibitors on either side who bugged out. But if you give me what I need right now, I promise no one will know that we spoke."

She nodded her head slowly, considering the options. A few moments later, she pulled a large black binder out of her top desk drawer and dropped it in front of him.

"You've been honest with me, Nash. I appreciate that." She flipped through the binder's loose-leaf pages until she came to a section headed Complaints.

"We're in luck," she said. "According to this, only one exhibitor failed to return yesterday. We logged three complaints on it. Whenever we have a skip, the companies around the empty booth are furious. Ruins the high-tech illusion, you know. They squawk early and often. We'd know by now about any other no-shows."

"So, who is it?" Nash leaned forward and tried to read the page upside-down.

"A real small fry," Harrison said. "Company name, Advance Tech, Inc. Product, photo CD albums. Exhibitor name, Andrew Bond. Local address, Lake Point Tower. What is that, an industrial park of some kind?"

Nash shook his head. "It's that rounded glass apartment

building on the lake a few miles north of here."

"Kind of strange to list an apartment as your company headquarters, don't you think?" Harrison said.

"I doubt that Mr. Bond is losing any sleep over it."

"Oh my, I guess you're right. Would you mind passing along any stories you write about this? I'd be very curious to know if the man's death had any connection to our show."

"Sure thing, Judy. And thanks."

"Any time, Nash. Don't be a stranger."

He found Povaric yelling at an old man behind the show's registration desk. Judging by the newspaper ripped up at his friend's feet, Nash guessed the piece on CTA fraud hadn't been deemed a valid press credential.

"But I'm telling you, I wrote the fucking story," Povaric was saying when Nash came within earshot.

"I don't get paid enough to listen to that kind of foul talk," the old man said. He was gripping the laminate desktop so hard his knuckles had turned white.

"Call my editors," Povaric demanded. "They'll tell you who I am."

"Buster, if I pick up that phone, it's going to be to call the cops," the man replied.

"Let's get out of here before he has a heart attack," Nash whispered.

"Christ, what do I need, a goddamn note from my mother?"

"Come on, I got everything we came for," Nash said, pulling on Povaric's sleeve as the old man picked up the phone and began punching in the code for building security.

"Okay, okay." The transit reporter pulled himself free of Nash's hand. Then he straightened his tie and yanked the cord out of the back of the phone. As Povaric stalked away, the registration attendant picked up the disconnected phone unit and threw it at him.

"Punks!" the man yelled as Nash and Povaric sprinted for the parking lot. "Bunch of goddamn punks!"

Chapter Eleven

Nash and Povaric entered the Cape Cod room of the Drake Hotel at exactly 12:03 p.m. After scanning the bustling room for a minute, Nash spotted Reg Devonshire and metro editor Phil Silvestri at a table overlooking North Michigan Avenue and Lake Shore Drive. They were ordering their meals.

"Can you believe that guy?" Povaric asked as they made their way to the table. "I knew he was a prick, but this really takes the cake."

"Ah, it's the Nash and Jerry show," Devonshire said as he handed his menu to the waiter.

"Hi, guys," Silvestri said, giving them an apologetic smile. "Do you need a minute to look at the menu?"

"What are your specials?" Nash asked the waiter as he and Povaric settled in.

"Might I recommend our fresh fillet of salmon wrapped in a light pastry shell and smothered with a rich béarnaise?"

"You might," Povaric said.

"Sounds good to me, too," Nash said.

"Would you also care for a tureen of spicy turtle soup as an appetizer?"

"We would," Povaric said.

"And to drink?"

Povaric glanced at Devonshire, who was clearly upset at the brutal assault being mounted on his expense account.

"Glenfiddich on the rocks, to start," Povaric said, looking to Nash for approval. "Make that two."

The waiter recorded their order in flowing shorthand. "Perhaps I could suggest a bottle of sauvignon blanc with your meal?"

"By all means," Silvestri said.

Nash broke into a broad grin. It would be harder for Devonshire to complain if they all got in on the act. And it served the managing editor right; only a true asshole would invite his subordinates to one of the classiest restaurants in town and then expect them to order off the value menu.

"Anything else, gentlemen?"

"That will be all," Devonshire said curtly. "Now, let's get to work so we can justify this lavish expenditure, shall we?" He finished with a tight smile, trying to pass his peevish statement off as a joke. The attempt did not succeed.

Nash pulled out the preliminary outline he'd put together that morning and shared his thoughts with the group. Silvestri and Povaric gave their hearty assent to his proposal. Within half an hour, they'd finished laying out a plan of attack.

Throughout the discussion, Devonshire remained strangely quiet. At first, Nash thought he wasn't participating because he was out of his depth, but as the work plan evolved, it became apparent the managing editor had been paying close attention.

As Nash emptied the last of the wine into Silvestri's glass, Devonshire dabbed at the corners of his mouth with a red cloth napkin and cleared his throat.

"I believe you have developed a reasonable strategy to investigate this murder," he began. "However, I am not sure that it goes quite far enough to give the story the impact Mr. Graf wants it to have."

"I'm eager to hear any suggestions," Nash said as he mopped up a pool of béarnaise sauce with a pumpernickel roll.

"I think you should spend some time in the city's homeless community," Devonshire said.

Povaric laughed so loud that diners at the three nearest tables turned around to see what had happened. "You don't mean he should go undercover and make a fool out of himself like Wilton Jasperson did?"

Jasperson, a local TV commentator, had recently dressed in raggedy clothes and trailed a camera crew behind him for three days while he tried to meet real homeless people and panhandle change on some of the city's busiest street corners. He had ended up a laughingstock of Chicago journalism, and all he had to show for his humiliation were three reports showing that, hey, it was pretty tough being a homeless guy.

"I didn't suggest that at all," Devonshire said. "Please hear me out. I think Nash should just be himself, no Salvation Army costumes or anything of the sort. But if you spend some time on the streets, you might be able to gain the trust of a few people. Enough, perhaps, to help you find out more about the victim's life and times prior to his final moments in that dreadful parking garage."

There was no argument that Reg Devonshire was an insufferable prick, but Nash had to admit his idea had considerable merit. Not only might it help him glean information pertinent to the murder investigation, the trip would give him the true-life horror stories he needed to spur his readers into action.

"I'll do it," Nash said. "After I complete the preliminary investigation."

He became so intrigued with the idea, he didn't realize

until hours later that he'd forgotten to bring up the matter of his raise. Maybe Devonshire wasn't quite as dumb as he appeared.

They arrived back at the office around 2:30.

"Quite a meal, if you overlook the company," Povaric said. Nash was on hold, waiting to speak to the detective in charge of the O'Hare killing.

"Ask him if they've got any suspects."

"Thanks, Jerry. I never would have thought of that one on my own."

"Just trying to be helpful."

"Next time you get the urge, why don't you . . . Hello? Yes. Thanks for speaking with me on such short notice. Yes. I'm calling about the killing yesterday at O'Hare. I wanted . . . Oh, I hadn't heard that. Could you at least give me the victim's name? I realize the position you're in here, but . . . Yes, nice talking to you, too . . ."

"I'm sorry I ever doubted your interviewing skills," Povaric said when Nash hung up. "That was a real clinic you put on just now."

"Something weird is happening on this one, Jerry."

"Do tell."

"Our friend in Homicide says the FBI took over the case. He can't give us any more help."

"His hands are tied?"

"Gee, were you listening in on the extension?"

"Why'd you ask the victim's name? That's the one piece of information we already have."

"I wanted to see how complete the blackout really is."

"It looks pretty dark from where I'm standing." Povaric sat on the corner of his desk and began rolling his tie up into a small tube.

"Don't give up yet." Nash grabbed his partner's coat from the back of a chair and handed it to him.

"Where to?" Povaric asked as he let his tie fall back into its normal shape.

"Lake Point Tower. Let's see how quickly our friends at the Federal Bureau of Investigation got out of the batter's box on this one."

Although the glittering round structure known as Lake Point Tower prides itself on being one of the city's most exclusive addresses, Nash and Povaric had no problem convincing the manager to take them to Andrew Bond's apartment. They simply told him the FBI wanted coverage of an important sting operation.

"That's the one," the man told them excitedly. "Sixteen F, end of the hall on your left."

"You'd better keep a safe distance," Nash told the manager when he began following them down the hall. "You wouldn't want to foul up any evidence."

Povaric was the first one to the door, what was left of it.

"I guess they beat us to the punch," he said, stepping over the splintered remains into the professionally tossed apartment.

"Let's sniff around a little anyway," Nash said. "You never know what might turn up. Like this." He picked a half-torn photo off the floor. A man and a woman were toasting the camera with tropical drinks at the beach. The man, outfitted in Hawaiian print shirt and blue-and-white striped walking shorts, looked like he had Eastern European roots. The woman, short and chesty with horse teeth and a permanent tan, looked like the only roots she cared about were the ones growing out of her scalp.

"That's the guy," Povaric said.

"We've got our front-page art," Nash said. "Now we need a story to go with it."

"I can't imagine the feds left anything behind for us to play with."

"Then you don't have a very big imagination, Jerry. Think about this for a second. Eastern European guy gets killed at the airport. Let's say, just for the sake of argument, he's Russian. All of a sudden, we've got the FBI involved in the investigation, and nobody's talking to the press."

"You think he might have been a spook?"

Nash touched his nose. "Give the man a prize. And the feds may have gone into this search not knowing Andrew Bond had been posing as a businessman."

Povaric shook his head. "The cops told me yesterday he was exhibiting at the electronics show."

"Okay, they know he's an exhibitor, but maybe they don't bother to find out exactly what he was selling before they ransacked the place."

"Because they figure it doesn't matter—they'll find everything hidden in here anyway."

"But we know what he was selling," Nash said, smiling.

All of a sudden, the light bulb clicked on inside Povaric's brain. "Albums for photo CDs."

Andrew Bond's entertainment center looked like it had been left out in a hurricane. His tape deck, CD player, tuner and amplifier had been pulled off their shelves and thrown savagely to the floor. Two full racks of compact discs, all featuring classical titles, were strewn over half the living room. Nash and Povaric got down on their knees and opened the CD jewel boxes one by one, discarding the ones with real music in them as they went along. When they finished, a stack of three disc boxes sat between them.

"I can't believe they were stupid enough to overlook

CD-ROMs, for chrissakes," Povaric said. "These guys are supposed to be our best and brightest."

"They apparently forgot the value of good backgrounding." Nash scooped up the discs and the torn photo on his way out.

"Is it safe to go in there yet?" the manager called from his vantage point behind the stairwell door.

"Yeah," Povaric said as he and Nash boarded the elevator. "I think the investigators got everything they needed."

Chapter Twelve

The police identified the murdered homeless man by sending his fingerprints through the National Criminal Information Center. Thanks to Avery Graf's intervention, the detective in charge gave Nash a full report.

The transient's name was Maynard Pike and he had a long criminal record. Born September 23rd, 1957, in Winston-Salem, North Carolina, Pike served time in juvenile detention for grand theft auto, vandalism and statutory rape. After his release, he became a drifter. Pike was tagged with minor charges in at least seven states, ranging from shoplifting and vagrancy to contributing to the delinquency of minors and trespassing. The highlights of his career included short stints in prison for breaking and entering, unarmed robbery and, again, statutory rape. And now he was dead.

No wives, children or other next-of-kin were listed on the rap sheet, and Nash imagined it would be difficult to track down the man's relations in North Carolina. After all, Pike had left the state in 1975 and, from the looks of things, his family had probably been eager to forget him. Ancient history like that wouldn't do much for the story anyway, so he decided to concentrate on Pike's Chicago days. But if Graf wanted to see an outpouring of compassion toward the homeless from the *Sentinel*'s readers after this series, he should have picked a nicer guy to focus on. This was going to be one bitch of a story to write.

Nash rubbed his temples and looked up at the hands on the newsroom's giant Art Deco wall clock. It was near enough to quitting time that he didn't feel guilty about heading home for a much-needed nap. Besides, he wanted to look at Andrew Bond's snapshot collection from his home computer. That had to count as work.

He waved at Povaric, who was working the phone trying to finish a story on expressway construction, then ducked into the back stairway to make a quiet exit.

The phone rang as Nash finished booting up his PC and checking his junk E-mail. He grabbed the receiver one ring before the answering machine picked up.

"I thought I was going to have to leave another embarrassing message there for a second," Samantha said.

"Hey sweet thing." Nash felt some of the day's tension lift off his shoulders. "I was just thinking about you."

"That's what they all say."

"I got your message last night. I liked it."

"I'm glad, Nash, but don't remind me of it. I felt so silly."

"It's always tough to let your guard down with a person for the first time. But I really appreciated it."

"And now it's your turn."

"Would you like to come up to my place tonight?"

"That would be nice. I always like to check in on my patients after I operate."

"I'm sure Cyd will be ecstatic to see you." Nash gave her directions.

"I'll be up in an hour or so. How does Chinese take-out sound?"

"You spoil me."

"Well, I expect something in return."

"I always pay my debts."

"See you soon, lover."

Nash poured a light Wild Turkey over his last three ice cubes and began scanning through the three CDs. They were filled with face shots of men and women on a trade show floor. He guessed the pictures had been taken from Andrew Bond's booth at the winter electronics exhibition in Atlanta; he wouldn't have had time to set up discs from the Chicago show so quickly. There were about ninety photos in all, but Nash didn't recognize any of the people in them. One of the subjects, an older man with a buzz cut and military bearing, looked vaguely familiar, but he couldn't quite place him. Other than that, he drew a blank.

The photos must have been advertised as some kind of premium at the booth. Try our digital camera and receive a photo of yourself on CD-ROM, something like that. They probably also served as insurance for Bond against being killed in his own exhibit. If the spy theory held true, most of these people were probably simply curious electronics buyers; but a few of them could have been conducting some rather specialized business with the booth's proprietor.

Samantha arrived after Nash started going through the discs for the third time, still with no luck.

"I got us some cashew chicken," she said when he opened the door. She wore a flimsy floral print summer dress that made her look several years younger.

"Smells good," he said, leaning forward to kiss her. "Doesn't taste too bad, either."

"Whatcha doing?" Sam asked as he grabbed plates and silverware. He explained the investigation while she dished up the meal.

"Would you mind taking a look at one guy for me? I

think he might be some well-known military man, but I can't come up with a name." Nash clicked through the disc, trying to find Mr. Brush Cut's picture.

"Wait a second," Sam said. "Go back one."

"That's not the guy," he said, flipping to a photo of a middle-aged man in a blue suit.

"But I know him. At least I know of him. That's Dr. Frederic Hintz. He's a bigwig research professor at the University of Illinois-Chicago. Of course, I studied on the Champaign-Urbana campus, but every veterinary student in the country knows about his work."

"Are you sure it's him?"

She bit her lip and nodded. "Pretty sure. He's big in the field."

"Fantastic. This really calls for a celebration," Nash gave her shoulders a squeeze. "You've given me the first living lead in this investigation."

"I do what I can." This time, Samantha leaned over to kiss him.

Chapter Thirteen

When Nash arrived at the newsroom Friday morning, he called his friend Curt Escobar at the San Bernardino *Ledger*. Nash had hooked Curt into an investigation that almost got him killed. But he'd also helped hook him up with features editor Faye Krashenko, who soon became his wife. That had to be good for a favor or two.

"Rambler!" Escobar said, using the nickname he'd bestowed upon Nash. "Things just haven't been the same since you left. How about coming back to stir things up a bit?"

"I've got the blenders on high right where I am, Curt."

"And I'm guessing you didn't just call me to commiserate."

"In fact, I do need a favor."

"I'd be surprised if I could be of much help to you up there in the City of Hog Shoulders, but I'll try."

"That's Big Shoulders, Curt."

"Pigs have big shoulders?"

Nash could hear Curt biting down on something, undoubtedly one of his beloved Twinkies. "Never mind," he said. "Look, I need some background on a man who was murdered at O'Hare this week."

"I see," Escobar mumbled, still chewing.

"The FBI clamped the lid down tight a few hours after the murder. I think the victim might have been KGB."

"He'd have to be ex-KGB now; there's been nothing left of that outfit since Gorbachev fell."

"Whatever. If I send a photo of this guy, do you think you might be able to tap some of your police sources to run a background check, tell me who he really is?"

"I'll give it a shot. But I can't promise anything."

"Thanks, Curt."

"Don't mention it. If I can get you any documentation, I'll send it Fed-Ex."

"Thanks, buddy."

"By the way, Faye and I were just talking about you a few days ago. She thinks it's about time for you to settle down. I don't know, though. If you did, I couldn't call you Rambler anymore."

"I don't think you've got anything to worry about for a while." Still, Nash couldn't help smiling at the thought of starting a life with Sam as he hung up the phone.

After spending the rest of his morning wrangling autopsy photos of Maynard Pike and Andrew Bond from an acquaintance at the Cook County Coroner's Office, Nash overnighted the Bond photos to Curt Escobar. At about 1:00, he grabbed a quick slice at a Union Station pizza stand with Jerry Povaric, who was still trying to juggle his transportation beat with the two murder investigations.

"I'm free for the rest of the afternoon," Povaric said between bites of pepperoni. "This Amtrak story I'm working on isn't due until next Tuesday."

"Then I think we should pay a visit to Dr. Frederic Hintz at the University of Illinois School of Veterinary Medicine," Nash said.

"What, you need a check-up or something?"

"His photo was on one of the CDs. I'm hoping Dr.

Hintz might be able to give us a reason why a Chicago animal researcher would be at an Atlanta consumer electronics show talking to a man selling cheesy photo albums."

"I'm sure there's a reasonable explanation," Povaric said.

"If nothing else, it should be an entertaining conversation."

They found Hintz hunched over a microscope in a cramped laboratory at the University of Illinois Circle Campus on the near West Side. White-coated lab assistants flitted about the room, preparing slides, mixing compounds and generally making themselves useful to the good doctor. When Hintz paused for a moment to clean his glasses, Nash introduced himself as a science reporter.

"And this is Jerry Povaric," Nash continued. "He writes a pet column for the paper and asked to come along for the ride."

"What a pleasant surprise," Hintz said, removing a pair of rubber gloves so he could shake their hands. "It's not often the local press takes an interest in our work here."

"From what we've heard, Doctor, that's a situation we really must rectify."

"Truly?" Hintz mused. "What have you heard?"

"About the breakthrough in veterinary medicine you're working on, of course," Povaric said.

"Yes, yes, I wasn't sure anyone outside the medical community had any knowledge of the new technique. I haven't yet published any papers on it, you see."

"Your colleagues around the city speak very highly of your work," Nash said.

"That's always nice to hear." For a moment, the doctor surveyed the laboratory distractedly. He was obviously eager to get back to work, but he seemed intrigued by the idea of getting some publicity as well. Finally, he put a hand on Nash's forearm and directed them into the hall.

"Please excuse my poor manners, gentlemen," he said. "Would you care to join me in my office for a cup of tea?"

"That would be most pleasant," Povaric said. The clipped speech pattern he affected almost made Nash laugh. As the doctor led them down the long, wood-paneled hallway, Nash elbowed his friend in the ribs. Povaric smiled and nudged right back, clearly enjoying his less-than-clever ruse.

"I don't want to keep you gentlemen here all afternoon," Hintz said as he poured them each a cup of Earl Grey. "So why don't you tell me what you need to know. That way I won't ramble so much."

"Could you start by giving us a brief overview of your current research and the progress you've been making?" Nash asked.

"Certainly," the doctor said, leaning back in his cracked leather chair. "As you may have heard, I have always directed my research toward finding cures for infectious animal diseases; cures that might someday help the medical community develop treatments for their human counterparts. My latest project is no different. I am pleased to report we are making great strides in the battle against the feline acquired immune deficiency virus."

"Kitty AIDS?" Povaric asked.

"Quite. The hope is that, in the process, we may also gain a better understanding of the human version of the virus."

"This is important work you're doing, Doctor," Nash said. He was impressed. "What kind of progress have you made?"

"The results thus far have been encouraging," Hintz said. "We actually had something of a major breakthrough in February. If we have discovered what I think we have discovered, we will publish a detailed scientific paper on our findings by early next year."

"Wow," Povaric said. "Could you give us a hint of things to come?"

"Although we have by no means completed all the necessary trials, we may have found a way to stimulate the growth of CD4 white blood cells, which are instrumental in combating the virus. The cells are, in essence, the main weapon of the body's immune system. In both cats and humans."

"So you believe the results could help further human AIDS research?" Nash asked.

"Yes. That is our fervent hope."

"Perhaps we'd best wait to do a story on your work until you've completed all the double-checking," Nash said.

"I think that would be the most prudent course of action." Hintz finished his tea and pushed back his chair. "Now if you will be kind enough to excuse me, I'll get back to the drawing board, as it were."

"Just one more question," Nash said.

"By all means," Hintz said as he stood and opened the door.

"You said your most recent breakthrough came in February."

"Yes."

"I was just wondering if that breakthrough might have had anything to do with your trip to Atlanta the month before."

The doctor's cordial smile disappeared. He closed the door and turned to face them. "I'm not sure I know what you're talking about."

"I'm sure you do, Dr. Hintz," Nash continued. "I'm talking about your meeting with Andrew Bond at the winter National Electronics Exhibition."

"Yes?" The doctor's face was ashen.

"Maybe you should sit down, Doc," Povaric said.

"No. I'll be fine. Look, whoever you really are, I have nothing further to say. And I'd like you to get the hell out of my office." He yanked the door open and glared at Nash and Povaric as they made their way into the hall.

"And if you harbor any ideas about coming back here to nose around, you should keep in mind an important lesson I've learned from my years of feline research," Hintz called after them.

"Curiosity killed the cat?" Povaric asked.

"That's the one."

"You may be right," Nash replied, "but I seem to remember hearing that satisfaction brought him back. We'll be in touch, Dr. Hintz."

Chapter Fourteen

He wished he could be doing something cozy and romantic with Samantha. He wished he could sit down in a big comfortable chair and rest a while. He wished Reg Devonshire's idea of spending time in the homeless community hadn't been such a good one. But here it was, Friday night, and Nash found himself squatting next to a small trash-can fire on the south bank of the Chicago River when he could have been drinking some good bourbon, eating some good food, making some good love. Ah, the trials of journalism.

"What paper you say you're from again?" the young black man on the other side of the can asked, his face lit up only occasionally by pieces of burning garbage floating out of the can.

"*Daily Sentinel*, Luther. Would you like a smoke?"

Nash saw the silhouette of a shaking head in the darkness. "Nah, man. I can't afford that habit."

"I'll take one, if you're offering." It was the old white man who called himself Wheezer. He let loose a wet, ragged cough that lasted almost a full minute.

"Sure," Nash said. "Anyone else?" He passed the pack around the circle, and was surprised to find several cigarettes left when it came back to him. *No thieves here,* Nash thought. He had not expected to find much decency in a hobo town, or whatever they called transient communities these days, but here it was.

"Do the cops hassle you much down here?" Nash asked. The ring of wooden palettes and cardboard boxes sat underneath the Michigan Avenue Bridge at the edge of Chicago's network of underground streets.

"Not since the Lower Wacker reconstruction finished up," a woman named Billie told him. "They know we don't have anyplace else to go." A frail, grandmotherly type with a tough, squinty glare, she was one of the most talkative members of the group.

"Whenever we go up into the world," Wheezer said, referring to the above-ground portion of the Loop, "the cops are the ones that make us come back down here."

"That's only if you stand around panhandling and making a scene," Luther said. "They don't mind it when we go for food at the shelters."

"It's still a free country," Wheezer interrupted. "A man ought to be able to walk around wherever he wants."

"Shit, old man, nobody wants you coughing and hacking all over them when they're waiting for the light to change," Luther countered. "It's downright unsanitary."

"Listen to that bickering, would you?" Billie said. She chuckled as she rocked back and forth on her heels. "They just fight to keep warm. You orter see us in the wintertime, Lord, we have to keep up the bickering all night long sometimes."

Ray, a quiet fat man hovering on the border between youth and middle age, moved into the light and looked carefully into Nash's eyes. "I've slept underneath your paper a time or two," he said. "But I don't remember ever seeing your name. How do we know you are who you say you are?"

"Yeah," Wheezer agreed, a paranoid look coming into

his eyes. "How are we supposed to know?"

"Now look what you've done, Ray," Luther said. "He'll be crazy scared all night because of you. Shit, you don't even know how to read."

"Do so," Ray said.

"Oh yeah?" Luther picked up a flattened oatmeal box. "Then read this."

Ray grabbed the box out of Luther's hand and tossed it into the river like a Frisbee. "It's too dark to read, fool," he said.

"Do you think it's too dark to maybe look at a picture for me?" Nash asked them. After a moment, Billie sidled up next to him.

"You gonna show us your family, maybe?" she asked. "You got a family don't you, Nash?"

"Yes, I've got a family, parents anyway. They live down in Florida now. Retired."

"I've been to Florida," Wheezer said. "Too hot."

"You wouldn't know Florida if it jumped up and bit your dick off," Ray said.

"Least I still got one to bite."

"I'll look at your picture," Luther said. He stood up to reveal a gangly, six-foot-four frame covered with an ancient velour sweatsuit. "Hand it over."

Soon enough, they had smoked the last of the cigarettes and considered the picture carefully. After all, it was the most exciting conversation piece of the evening. Nash could see by the expressions on their faces as they passed it around that the photo of a dead Maynard Pike lying on a stainless-steel operating table reminded them all too much of their own mortality.

"I've seen this man," Wheezer said, handing the picture back to Nash. "His handle was Pete."

"I ain't seen him," Ray said. "And I bet he hasn't either."

"Yes I have," Wheezer insisted.

"I might'a seen him around, too," Billie said. "At the Division Street Mission. I think he used to take his meals there in the spring. I can't recall seeing him there lately, though."

"Was his name Pete?" Wheezer asked.

"I don't really know. I can't recall if I ever spoke to him or not." Billie shook her head, then began to cry. "It's just horrible to see one of us die like that. You expect to die of cold or heat. You expect to die of bitterness, or hunger, or exhaustion. But no one deserves to be murdered in cold blood like that."

"No one deserves to be down here, period," Nash said. "The more I can find out about this man's life here in Chicago, the more likely it is I can figure out who killed him. And maybe, the stories I write will move people to help solve this whole damn situation." He paused and looked up at the sky cut into tiny sections by the downtown skyscrapers. The glow of the city's bright lights had blocked out all the stars. "Maybe. But probably not."

"Pike," Luther said quietly.

"What's that?" Nash asked.

"Pike. The man's name was Pike."

"Are you sure it wasn't Pete?" Wheezer asked, scratching thoughtfully at his long gray beard. "Because I'm sure I remember somebody calling him Pete."

"Did you know him?" Nash asked.

"Well enough to stay away from him," Luther said.

"Was he violent?"

"You better believe it. I wasn't afraid of him, you understand, but I've got enough problems without having to deal with some psychotic bullshit like that."

"Did he hang out with anyone?"

"Yeah. He had a buddy. Guy by the name of Virgil. He's just as bone crazy as Pike was."

"You think it's possible they might have had a fight that left one of them dead?"

"Possible?" Luther laughed. "Shit, I'm surprised it didn't happen a lot sooner than this."

"Can you tell me where this Virgil might be holing up?" Nash asked.

"I can tell you a couple of places, but you'll have to find them on your own. Virgil's the kind of guy, once he gets a taste of killing, he's liable to take it up as a hobby."

Chapter Fifteen

After Luther gave him a description of the man named Virgil and a list of probable hangouts, Nash decided he'd had enough of life on the streets for one night. He needed a long, hot shower and lots of booze. Enough, at least, to wash away the memory of the transient camp for the night.

He understood, to a certain extent, why most people ignored the homeless whenever they could; it was unbearable to think about such horribly wasted lives for any length of time. Because these transients shattered a person's illusion that the world somehow made sense, that things happened for a reason, that America was the land of opportunity, they were simply cut from the script of everyday existence. And Nash had just spent the better part of an evening exploring the pieces on the cutting room floor.

Driving home, he felt so weary he wasn't sure if he would be able to stay awake long enough to rinse the shampoo out of his hair, let alone take a long shower. Maybe the hot, clean water would revitalize him enough to give Samantha a call before bed.

When he opened the door and saw Elizabeth Dade Pulliam sleeping on his couch, however, he suddenly felt like he'd been given a shot of pure adrenaline. He closed the door softly in front of him and remained in the hallway for a long moment, breathing deeply to slow his racing heartbeat and trying to decide if he'd just had some kind of hallucination.

"Nash, is that you?"

Elizabeth's sleepy voice on the other side of the door brought him back to reality. His first instinct was to flee to the safety of Samantha's apartment; he didn't need this kind of complication in his life right now.

"Nash, come on," Elizabeth called. "You're scaring me."

He opened the door and was taken aback by how excited he was to see her there, stretching and yawning like a cat. The large gray eyes and wispy, shoulder-length brown hair he had woken up to see almost every morning during the past two years were exactly the same as he remembered them. The low, mellow sound of her voice, the knowing half-smile—nothing about her seemed to have changed. When she stood and gave him a long, enveloping hug, he whispered the only words that came to mind.

"Welcome home."

He hated himself in the morning, of course. They hadn't spoken more than a dozen words all night, yet they had somehow managed to become fully reacquainted. As he lay with his eyes closed in the rumpled bed he had shared so recently with another woman, Nash listened to the distant drumbeat of the shower and imagined himself alone in a tropical rain forest, far away from any other human beings whose lives he could fuck up.

Throwing on his robe, Nash picked his way through the trail of discarded clothes leading from the bedroom to the living room and gave Thucydides his morning meal.

"Men are scum," he said as he measured out a dish full of seeds. "We do not deserve the happiness we receive."

Somewhere behind that almost overwhelming wall of

guilt, however, Nash was secretly glad that Elizabeth had returned to him. She had seen the error of her ways, found that she could not live without his touch. Vindication was his. Certainly, he should have turned her away once he'd had the satisfaction of knowing about her change of heart, but his judgment had been impaired by a combination of shock, fatigue and despair.

"Fuck the justifications, Cyd," he said as he filled the squirrel's water tank. "Fact is, I let the little head think for the big one again. When will I ever learn?"

"Never, I hope."

He turned to see Elizabeth wrapped in a fluffy white towel that barely covered enough of her clean pink skin, a vision straight out of his tortured imagination.

"I knew you'd come back," he said, flashing an ironic grin.

"The hell you did."

She walked across the room and pressed her body tightly against his. He moved his hands to the bottom of the towel and slid it up to the middle of her back, then lowered his head to kiss the base of her neck. She began to say something, but caught her breath when he began to nibble gently on her earlobe.

"If you were sure I'd be running back into your arms, why the hell did you get rid of every gift I ever gave you?" she whispered in his ear before playfully pushing him away.

He rubbed the tickle of her breath away. "You noticed that, huh?"

"Like you, I'm very observant." She gestured at the squirrel lounging in his cage. "For instance, I also noticed you've turned your apartment into a wildlife sanctuary."

Over toaster waffles and microwaved bacon, he told her

the story of Cyd and the shooting gallery of love he'd created to exorcise his break-up pain.

Laughing, she leaned across the kitchen table and swiped a dab of syrup off his cheek with a perfectly manicured index finger. Even wrapped in nothing more than a big bath towel, she managed to embody poise and elegance. "So melodramatic, Nash! And all because of me? I love it." She sucked the syrup drop into her mouth with a wet, sexy pop.

He felt himself blush. "Well, I'd been drinking."

"Also because of me. Face it: You could barely live without me. I'm surprised you still have both your ears."

"I wasn't drinking absinthe."

"No, it's always bourbon with you, tough guy. I climbed into the bottle for a few days there myself. Several bottles of Yellow Label, in fact, with nary a glass in sight. Breaking up with you was the hardest thing I've ever done. It did seem like the logical thing to do, though. My life's been expanding so far beyond Chicago, I just felt I needed to be free to grab any opportunity that came my way."

"Don't rake me over the coals again. I'm almost out of Wild Turkey."

"I'm not breaking up with you again, silly." She took his hands and pulled him up into a full embrace. "I'm trying to tell you how much I missed you," she said finally, "and that I was wrong. I want us to get a place together, Nash. I want to be with you."

"Oh, God." He released his grip on her and backed away. "I don't know if I can shift gears this quickly."

"It's fine with me if you need a few days to let it all sink in." Elizabeth let the towel drop and stood before him, a dream lover come back to life. A few beads of condensation clung to the bottoms of her small, firm breasts, and Nash

110

got an erection in spite of himself.

"But the longer you take to make up your mind," she added, "the longer you have to do without this."

"Why are you coming on so strong all of a sudden?" He couldn't help staring at her; until last night, he didn't imagine he'd ever see her again—especially like this.

"I feel terrible for all the pain I've put you through." She took a step toward him. "I'm just trying to make it up to you. I thought you'd be happy."

"I am happy. But it's not that simple."

"You're still mad at me. Believe me, I don't blame you. I was pretty upset with myself there for a while. I got scared and I panicked and I did something really stupid. Please forgive me, Nash. I want us to be happy together. I could come back to Chicago. Or you could move to L.A."

"It's just not that simple," he repeated, more to himself than to her.

"Why?"

"I'm involved with another woman."

His stomach turned as the words left his mouth, bringing into the open a reality he had tried so hard to deny for the last six hours. As he spoke, the air in the room became somehow thinner, chillier. Elizabeth felt it too, he thought as he watched her cover herself back up with the towel and retreat into the bedroom to retrieve her things. This time, he knew, he had really gotten himself into a jam.

But when Nash spotted Samantha's car pulling up in front of the apartment building a few moments later, he had a sinking feeling he might find his love life becoming a lot less complicated any minute now.

Chapter Sixteen

He hurried down to the porch, drawing the robe tight around his body, and waved at Samantha as she emerged from the car.

"I'm surprised to see you awake this early after your night out with the homeless," she said.

"I couldn't sleep."

Sam walked up and gave him a short hug and kiss.

"You smell weird," she said.

"It must be left over from last night. I was too tired to shower when I got home."

"Hmmm. Smells more like stale perfume to me. And sex. You're not sleeping around on me already, are you?"

At that moment, Nash felt utterly helpless and alone.

"Hey, cheer up," Samantha said. "I'm only kidding." She looked down at her watch. "And running very late. I just stopped by to say hello on my way to work. Come see me at the clinic later today if you feel like it, okay?"

"Okay," he said. "Sam?"

"Yes, Nash."

"I want you to know, what you said on my answering machine the other night? I feel exactly the same way."

"Ah, that's nice, lover. I'm going to have to make you a regular stop on my morning commute."

As he watched her climb into her car and speed away, Nash knew that he had turned a corner in his life. For better or worse, he had left Elizabeth behind.

"Just consider last night a farewell fuck," she said when she found him on the porch a few minutes later. "I should have known better than to second-guess my instincts."

"Yeah," Nash said, "you're probably right." He looked into her tear-stained face and tried to commit every pore to memory. He'd enjoyed a brief reprieve last night, but this was really the end of the line. "At least now you'll be able to be mad at me for a while instead of feeling so guilty."

She laughed and sniffed at the same time. "That's true enough. Christ, Nash, why do you always have to be so goddamn charming?"

"And why do you have to always be so goddamn beautiful?"

"Hah!" she said, wiping some of the moisture off her cheek. "Now I know you're lying. Here I am after a five-hour flight, I've had no sleep, and now I'm crying. That's some prescription for beauty."

"Remember the first time we met, when I thought you were a model?"

"Yeah."

"That wasn't a line. I swear, Liz, you are one of the hottest women walking around on the planet. And one of the nicest companions, too."

The tears came to him now as well. They stood on the porch for a minute, sobbing like idiots in front of the heavy rush-hour traffic. Finally, she took his hand and pressed the spare set of apartment keys into his palm.

"I am going to miss you, Nash."

"The feeling is very, very mutual." He could barely force out the words.

Liz shook her head. "I don't know who's been stupider

about this—you or me."

She kissed him once on the forehead, and then walked back out of his life before the saliva even had a chance to dry.

Chapter Seventeen

He took a head-clearing jog up the Lake Michigan side of campus, pumped up on the guilty adrenaline of cheating on Samantha and getting away with it. But even as his legs pushed him forward, Nash's mind kept taking him back to his one-night reunion with Elizabeth and the bittersweet relationship that had come before it.

One question kept nagging at him: If Liz had expressed second thoughts about breaking up before he met Sam, would he have been so quick to push her away? He suspected he would have welcomed Elizabeth back into his life, if warily. He would have needed time to put his trust in her again, so Nash was sure he would have rejected her idea of moving in together right away. But once he felt sure Elizabeth was really serious about coming back to him, he might have drifted off to Los Angeles and made a life with her.

And if that was the case, why had he rejected Elizabeth's offer out of hand? He and Sam hadn't been together long, after all, certainly not long enough for Nash to be making long-term plans with her. Was it simple spite, the sadistic enjoyment of unexpectedly having the upper hand after Liz broke up with him over the phone?

Nash stopped outside a fraternity house on Lincoln Street. Hands on his thighs, he took several deep breaths as he watched cars drive along the northern border of campus. It certainly had felt better to be the dumper than the dumped. Even so, he couldn't see himself throwing away a happy life with Elizabeth just to get back at her.

His gut had told him it was time to move on, and having Sam in his life made it easier to act on that instinct. It wasn't that he doubted he could rebuild his relationship with Liz. But he knew his ex well enough to sense that her attempt at reconciliation was driven more by fear and nostalgia than it was by a firm desire to get back together. Once she got comfortable on the West Coast, she probably would have cut him loose for good. Still, Nash knew he made a better reporter than pundit. What if his analysis was wrong?

Still breathing hard, he stood up as a cute undergrad in purple sweats and tousled black hair crept out of the house and then hurried past him on her walk of shame back to whatever dorm she called home. He'd never been a fan of one-night stands, but as he noticed the white Willie the Wildcat pawprints stenciled down the back of the shapely young woman's lavender pants, Nash had to smile at the thought that he had scored like a frat boy.

Except for a few hours spent reviewing the CD-ROMs with Jerry Povaric on Saturday afternoon—a futile effort, as the transit reporter hadn't been able to put any names to the faces either—Nash devoted the remainder of his weekend to rest and relaxation. He found that since his relationship with Liz had been more or less permanently resolved, he enjoyed his time with Samantha even more than he had the previous week.

They went to an old Rolling Stones concert movie at the Museum of Science & Industry Imax theater. They played with baby goats at the Brookfield petting zoo. They watched the White Sox destroy the Minnesota Twins in both halves of a magnificent double-header. They ate a lot more pasta and Ben & Jerry's ice cream. In short, Nash and Samantha had the kind of weekend that would be almost impossible to top.

Nash even got a major break in the Andrew Bond story without so much as lifting a finger. When they arrived back at his apartment after the Sox games, they found Thucydides running loose, the lid of his cage thrown wide open. Nash suspected he had failed to set the latch after his confrontation with Elizabeth.

It had taken Cyd a full day to realize he was only one hard push away from freedom, but he made up for his oversight in a hurry. Magazines, shoes, half-filled coffee cups—practically everything in the apartment that was not tied down had been knocked over, chewed on or, in many cases, both. It took Samantha almost fifteen minutes to grab the little bugger and calm him down enough to get him back in the cage.

"At least his stitches held," she said.

"Thank goodness for small favors," Nash said, wiping up one of the many spills in the kitchen. "Whenever you give him the Sam Parker seal of approval, I think old Cyd should go back into the wild."

They had nearly finished tidying up the mess when Nash noticed a silvery CD poking out from behind the TV. Cyd had apparently knocked the photo discs onto the floor and, in so doing, caused one of the jewel boxes to break apart. Nash retrieved it from behind the set and sat down on the couch to put it back together. As he snapped the tray into place, he saw a small piece of notebook paper sticking out from under it. He pulled apart the two bottom sections of the box. There, sandwiched between the dark plastic tray and the clear section holding the back cover of a Mahler concerto, sat a list of five names written in cramped Cyrillic

117

letters. The other two disc boxes held similar lists.

"Hey, Samantha," he said. "How does Sunday dinner at the Red Apple grab you?"

They found the smorgasbord even more crowded, if that was possible, than it had been the Monday before. After a fifteen-minute wait, they were seated in the friendly Kamil's section once again.

"Do you remember us from last week?" Nash asked as they sat down.

"Yes," Kamil said. "You drank Stoli like a real Pole."

"That's us. Kamil, do you think you might be able to do me a favor?"

"Depends. I'm very busy."

"Can you read Russian by any chance?"

Kamil frowned. "I try to forget as much as possible. We were required to learn Russian when Poland was under Soviet rule, but I was very young. I do not think I can help you."

"That's too bad," Nash said, pulling out the three scraps of notebook paper along with a twenty-dollar bill. "Because I need someone to translate a few names for me."

Kamil looked around quickly, then grabbed the papers from Nash's hand. "I think I will be able to do this on my next break. Now, can I bring you something from the bar before dinner?"

"Kamil, you are definitely my kind of waiter. I'll take a bourbon on the rocks. And Samantha here will have . . ."

"Gin and cranberry juice, if you have it."

Kamil nodded and made his way back to the bar half of the establishment, where several old men sat on padded stools, nursing beers and vodkas and watching a soccer match on a pair of vintage color TVs.

"So," Samantha began. "How was your week?"

"Not nearly as good as my weekend."

Samantha accepted her Sea Breeze from Kamil and pressed the frosted glass against her right cheek. "It's hot in here," she said.

"We'll take a walk by the lake after dinner to cool down a bit."

"That sounds romantic."

"How about your week? Did you save many lives?"

"A few. Actually, my most interesting patient was a tarantula."

"I thought you were supposed to step on those, not treat them."

"What a horrible thing to say. Kim was beautiful. She'll stay on your hand and let you pet her as long as you like."

Nash shivered. "I can't stand spiders."

"I'm sure you would have made an exception for this one. Nature comes up with so many interesting variations. I really love my work."

"We're both lucky in that regard," Nash said, raising his glass in a toast. "So what was Kimmy's problem? Spider hairball?"

"For your information, Mr. Hansen, she suffered from dehydration. I got some fluids into her and made an eleven-year-old boy extremely happy."

"Why would a little boy name a tarantula Kim? Doesn't seem appropriate somehow."

Samantha smiled. "Kim is his sister's name."

"That explains it." They finished their drinks and began slowly snaking their way through the monumental buffet line.

Nash grabbed Samantha a plate that felt like it had come straight out of the dishwasher. "The problem with waiting this long is that you're ravenous by the time you get to the food."

"I know," she said. "I always take too much when I come here."

When they were about ready to go back for seconds, Kamil emerged from the kitchen and waved a sheet of paper at them.

"Piece of cake," the young waiter said as Nash folded the list and stuffed it in his pocket. As he'd suspected, Dr. Frederic Hintz was one of the five names Andrew Bond had written down from the second disc.

"So the professor got himself involved in some risky business," Samantha said. "Somehow, I'm not surprised. He has a reputation for being more concerned with the scientific glory than the achievement."

"Yeah, he seemed delighted to talk to me and Jerry Povaric when he thought we'd be giving him some positive ink. I think he fancies himself the cock of the walk in his particular field."

"I might know someone else who feels the same way about his job."

"Hey," Nash said. "I'm just a humble man who tries to do the best damn work he can."

"Uh huh." She laughed. "You're fun to tease."

"I'm glad I can provide some amusement."

"It's a bad habit, I guess, teasing. Comes from being the oldest of five. Three sisters and a brother. The next-oldest is twenty-three. Jennifer."

"Three years apart?"

Samantha nodded. "And the youngest, William, he's only ten if you can believe it."

"Your parents must be insane."

"Mom can't stand an empty house. I grew up in a big

old woodframe in Bridgeport, Mayor Daley's neighborhood before he ditched it. Mom's always kept the place spotless, but she loves the sound of kids running around. Now she's pestering us girls to start giving her some grandchildren."

"And how do you feel about that?"

"I love kids. And now that I'm pretty well established in my career, that seems to be the next big step."

"I feel the exact same way."

"You're just saying that," she said, blushing.

"No. I mean it." They looked at each other without speaking for several beats. Nash was a little frightened by how perfect they were together after only a week.

"I think we'd better change the subject," Samantha said. "I'm beginning to feel a little silly."

"Me, too."

They hadn't noticed Kamil standing next to the table. If the grin on his face was any indication, he'd been there a while.

"You two are cute together," the waiter said. "Will you invite me to the wedding?" Samantha's blush grew deeper by the second.

"Don't you have better things to do than spy on your customers?" Nash asked.

"Sure. But none of them are this much fun. Would you like some iced Stoli now, perhaps?"

"Maybe next time," Nash said.

"Ah yes," Kamil said, giving them a broad wink. "I think *you* are the ones with better things to do. I'll get your check."

"Cheeky guy," Nash said once the waiter had left.

"I like him," Samantha said.

"You know what? I do, too."

"So why do you think Dr. Hintz met with your dead Russian spy?"

"My hunch is Hintz bought some kind of information that helped him complete his latest breakthrough, but I haven't quite put all the pieces together yet."

"Intellectual theft is something of a time-honored tradition among scientists," Samantha said as they paid the check and made their way to the BMW.

"Really?"

"Yep. Even the great Louis Pasteur pilfered some of his research."

"You're kidding."

She shook her head. "Apparently, Pasteur pronounced his rabies vaccine ready for testing when it was still more or less in the theoretical stage. Fortunately for him, a lesser-known French scientist had already developed an alternative method."

"Which Pasteur ripped off?"

"Right. When old Louis conducted the first public test of the vaccine by inoculating a small herd of sheep, he gave them the other scientist's treatment. A few months later, Pasteur discovered his theories were correct and from then on he only used the vaccine he had invented."

"What about the other scientist?"

"He went mad."

"Jeez, I'll never enjoy another glass of milk as long as I live," Nash said as he drove them toward the lake.

"Pasteurization is a whole different process, dummy."

"Still," Nash said, "this information comes as quite a blow."

Chapter Eighteen

Checking out the names from the CD-ROM lists proved to be a surprisingly simple exercise. Running them through the paper's computerized morgue files provided occupations and locations for nine of the fifteen people in Andrew Bond's notes; a scan of national and international *Who's Who* editions and a quick trip through Google supplied the rest.

All but two of the people from the lists worked for the U.S. and foreign governments. The other two were Dr. Hintz and Mr. Brush Cut himself. The man Nash hadn't quite been able to place last Thursday night was Canfield Davis, president of Midwest Avionics, Inc., a defense contractor in the northwest suburbs. Nash remembered seeing his picture two or three times before in the *Sentinel* business section.

Although most journalists considered such drudge work a necessary evil, Nash loved backgrounding sources and conducting library research almost as much as going out on the streets. Jerry Povaric, however, sided with the majority on this one. After an hour scanning through computer files and cross-referencing photos from back issues of the paper, the transit reporter looked as bored as a jock in trigonometry class.

Rather than listen to his complaints for the rest of the morning, Nash excused Povaric to check some of the sites where Maynard Pike's old roommate might be hanging out.

"If you see this Virgil character, call the cops for assistance," Nash said. "I told the detective in charge of the investigation what my homeless contact said about the guy's violent tendencies, so now the police are eager to ask him a few questions."

"Can I talk to him for a few minutes first?"

"Luther said he's a dangerous man, Jerry. Just find a pay phone and dial nine-one-one. Besides, Detective Coltraine promised he'll give us a full report on the interrogation if we cooperate."

"I guess I won't risk it then. If I see Virgil, I'll turn tail quick like a bunny rabbit and pick up a phone. Have fun in your electronic playground, Nash."

"If you know what's good for you, you won't come back to the office until after lunch. I should be just about finished by then."

He let out a low whistle when he matched Canfield Davis to his occupation. Nash didn't want to risk creating an international incident by putting the squeeze on any of the foreign agents on the list, but he imagined Davis might be able to provide him with several pertinent details in exchange for saving his own ass.

"I'd like to speak to Mr. Davis, please," Nash said when the company president's personal secretary picked up.

"Do you have an appointment?" the man asked.

"No, sir, I sure don't. I'm Nash Hansen from the *Daily Sentinel* and what I have to ask Mr. Davis will only take a minute."

"I can leave a message . . ."

"Tell you what," Nash continued in his most jocular tone. "I am sure Mr. Davis will want to drop what he's doing and take a moment to speak with me."

"And why would that be?"

"If he doesn't, a story will run in tomorrow's editions that will be a source of particular embarrassment to him."

"And if he speaks to you?"

"We just might be able to work something out. Why don't you buzz Mr. Davis on the intercom and tell him I'm calling to ask about his trip to the National Electronics Exhibition in Atlanta this January. He'll know what I'm talking about."

"Hold on one second, please."

The guy was all business; he'd expressed no personal curiosity, just cut right to the chase to see if a conversation with Nash Hansen would be in his boss' best interests. He guessed Canfield Davis had learned to surround himself with shrewd and loyal employees when he'd served eight years on the Joint Chiefs of Staff in the 1980s.

Davis used the connections forged during his long and distinguished military career to launch himself into business as a defense contractor at the end of the Reagan administration. With Reagan's penchant for $300 billion defense budgets, Midwest Avionics, Inc. soon found itself awash in government contracts. By 2004, only sixteeen years after Davis founded the company, MAI handled close to $300 million in contracts annually.

After about a five-minute wait, Davis came roaring onto the line.

"What is this bullshit, some kind of blackmail scheme?" he demanded. "I'll feed your bloody corpse to the sharks if you try and fuck me."

"Good afternoon to you too, Mr. Davis." Nash put just enough honey in his voice to show he wasn't going to back down that easily.

"Just tell me what the hell you want."

"I've got information linking you to Andrew Bond."

Davis paused. "Never heard of him," he said finally. "But just out of curiosity, who else knows about this?"

"No one else. So far."

"What's your pitch?"

"I want to know what Bond sold, who he sold it to, and how he got his wares. I also want details on how he set up his sales and any personal information you can give me about the man."

"And what will I get out of this transaction?"

"You're my Deep Throat," Nash said. "I'll quote you as an anonymous source and I won't include any information in my story that will implicate you directly. So, do we have a deal?"

"Call me at this number in exactly three hours. In the meantime, I'm going to consult with my attorney. If I agree to your proposition, he will be listening in on the conversation."

"You'll hear from me at two-fifteen. And I want to make this clear, Mr. Davis: If you don't cooperate with me, I'll be forced to go straight to the authorities."

"It's been a long time since I've met a man stupid enough to threaten me, Hansen. I sincerely hope you don't live to regret it."

"I'm touched by your concern." Before Davis had a chance to respond, Nash hung up.

He was glad there would be another person on Davis' end of the line; it would give him the chance to test an idea he'd been working on. He couldn't stay in the newsroom to attempt what he had in mind, however. He would need the electronic equipment he kept at his apartment. Nash called city editor Phil Silvestri to his desk and gave him a brief update on both investigations. Then he packed up the thick folder of information he'd accessed and got ready to head back to Evanston for the day.

As he stood to leave, Nash's extension rang. He thought about letting the voice mail pick up, but he didn't want to miss any calls from Povaric or the police. When he heard the voice of convention bureau president Gil Francis on the line, however, Nash wished he hadn't been so conscientious.

"How does it feel to have single-handedly cost the city thirty million a year in economic impact?" Francis asked.

"I'm sorry you're still mad at me, Gil. I think we both saw the handwriting on the wall before my story ran."

"But we'll never know, will we? If you had just let me postpone the discovery of that goddamn transient for two or three more days, then maybe, just maybe, public attendance at the electronics show wouldn't have dropped like a fucking rock over the weekend."

"And if wishes were horses, the streets would be covered with shit."

"The electronics association called me this morning, Nash. They're pulling the plug on the summer show for good."

"I'm sorry, Gil. I know you went to the mat on this one."

"You don't know the half of it. I promised my board I'd resign if I couldn't keep the show. I want you to know I hold you responsible for ending my career."

"I can't accept that responsibility, Gil. But I'm sorry just the same."

"Sorry's not good enough, Nash."

"I'm afraid it's going to have to be."

"Don't bet on it."

"What the hell's that supposed to mean?" Nash asked. But the harsh sound of the dial tone ringing in his ear was the only response he received.

Chapter Nineteen

When the kitchen clock clicked ahead to 2:15, Nash crossed his fingers and dialed Midwest Avionics, Inc. He'd installed a Web telephone program on his PC and downloaded a Muzak MP3, which was cued up now. He'd never been able to resist "The Girl from Ipanema." If the setup worked, he might be able to get some information that Canfield Davis would never dream of telling him.

"I'm putting you on the speaker phone, Nash," Davis said when the connection went through.

"Who's in the room with you?"

"My lawyer, Bill Hendricks. No one else."

"Fair enough. He's been apprised of the situation?"

"You may speak freely."

"First off, I'd like to know how Andrew Bond contacted Midwest Avionics, so I can get an idea of how he operated with the rest of his clients."

"Go ahead, Canfield," Hendricks said. "As long as this conversation stays on deep background."

"He sent me partial sketches, enough information to prove he had the goods."

"Why did he choose MAI over all the other defense aviation firms?"

"I have no idea. For all I know, he sent the same 'sales kit' to several different companies and I came out the highest bidder. If he was smart, that's just the way he did it."

"How did you submit your bid?"

"By mail, to a blind Chicago post office box. Bond was an extremely careful man."

"It seems he had reason to be."

"Yes," Davis said dryly.

"Were the plans he sold you designs for Russian armaments?"

"Yes."

"Did he deliver on his promises?"

"Oh, yes."

"Which gave you quite a jump on the competition, didn't it, Davis? A little free research and development."

"It was hardly free."

"Which brings us to our next question: How did you pay Bond?"

"He insisted on used twenties. It was a pain in the ass to put together that many of them."

"Did you send the money to the post office box, too?"

"No. We made the exchange at the electronics show. Dealing out in the open on neutral ground provided a comfort level for both parties."

"Less chance of a double-cross."

"Exactly."

"Did you ever see Andrew Bond after Atlanta?"

"No. Never. He'd already sold us everything useful he had."

"Did he tell you how he came across the information?"

"I never asked, he never volunteered. I assumed he was ex-KGB."

"Weren't you afraid it might be a sting?"

"I have enough friends in high places that I'd know about it before it came down around my ears."

"You sound pretty sure of your connections."

"They always provide decision-quality information."

"Do you know anything at all about Bond's private life?"

"He was well-dressed, a man of expensive tastes. In my estimation, that's a sign of weakness. Other than that, I know he had a thick Russian accent, sounded like a Muscovite to me. And that's all she wrote."

"Is this sort of arrangement common practice in defense circles?"

"Industrial espionage? It's a fact of life in every sector of business I'm familiar with. We're no different from the perfume industry, the auto industry, pharmaceuticals. You name it."

"Except, I believe, there are stricter laws regulating the purchase and sale of weapons of mass destruction."

"That's true," Davis said.

"I understood MAI's alleged involvement in any illegalities would not be the issue here," Hendricks said.

"Don't get your underwear all bound up," Nash said, "I was just making a distinction. Now how about telling me what you know about Bond's other clients."

"I have no knowledge of them," Davis said. "And I would expect they would have no knowledge of me. As I stated earlier, Bond was a very careful businessman."

"But not careful enough to avoid getting himself stabbed to death at the airport last week."

"What's your point?" Hendricks asked.

"I just want to find out where your client was when Andrew Bond died."

"My client . . ."

"Whoa," Nash interrupted. "Could you hold that thought for a moment? I've got another call coming in. Just let me put you on hold and get rid of it."

"Make it quick," Davis said.

"Will do."

Nash cut the mic and clicked play on the MP3. While the music played, the tape recorder next to the PC speaker recorded the open line. Nash turned up the volume.

"Canfield, if you killed Bond, I'd advise you to terminate this conversation and take immediate precautions," Hendricks said.

"Christ, Bill, why would I want to have him killed?"

"You said yourself that most of the plans he sold you were hopelessly out of date."

"That's the cost of doing business. Killing Bond would leave this company unnecessarily exposed."

"Where were you on the day of the murder, Canfield?"

"In Washington, meeting with members of the House Armed Services Committee about an F-16 engine contract."

"Then you're personally in the clear."

"For the last goddamn time, Bill, I didn't kill Andrew Bond and I didn't have him killed."

"I had to be sure," Hendricks said. "It's my job."

"No, your job is to make sure I stay out of harm's way whether I fucking did it or not."

Nash stopped the MP3 and turned his microphone back on, satisfied for the moment that Canfield Davis wasn't his man.

"Did what or not?" he asked.

"I'm finished talking with you, you little fuck. Go crawl back under your rock."

"Mr. Davis met with members of Congress in Washington on the day in question," Hendricks said.

"I'll be sure to check that out," Nash said.

"You do that," Davis snarled. "But if any part of this

story comes back to me, I'll give you another murder to worry about."

Nash cut the connection. The story was so close he could taste it. But he still needed to know who killed Andrew Bond.

Chapter Twenty

Nash took the rest of the afternoon off to catch up on his life. He made a shopping list and added a note to stop by Radio Shack to nose around for new recording technologies; he'd seen some interesting miniature tape recorders at the electronics show; a few of them might already be in stores. Before heading off to the supermarket, however, he walked across the street for a trim and some conversation at Freddy's Barbershop.

He was something of a celebrity at Freddy's, and in the rest of the neighborhood as well, due to the fact that he was one of very few white people living in the ten-block square north of Golf and west of Green Bay Road that comprised Evanston's main black section. He'd moved into the area as a student because the rents were cheaper. It hadn't seemed like a big deal to him; growing up on the border between Latin and Korean neighborhoods on Chicago's northwest side had prepared him well to accept his current outsider status.

He'd kept the apartment after graduation because the street was quiet, the neighbors were sociable and his building was old enough to have character, but not so old as to need constant repairs. Also, the two-flat was exactly a block away from two of his favorite restaurants: Buffalo Joe's, famous for its scorching "suicide" chicken wings, and Hecky's, a phenomenal barbecue joint that served fatback ribs the way God intended—with extra sauce, a mound of coleslaw and a healthy slice of sweet potato pie for dessert. When the wind blew just right, Nash could lean out his front window and catch a whiff of Hecky's sweet-smelling smoke.

"When you let your hair grow out, Nash, I swear you're just as nappy headed as most of the other kids in this neighborhood," Freddy said. He shook his head in amusement as he brushed off the shop's lone chair.

Nash rested against the green Naugahyde and Freddy went to work with a comb and spray bottle, trying to see what he had to work with. Nash closed his eyes and began to drift, but when the metallic drone of an electric razor filled the shop, he opened them abruptly.

"You want I should make this quick?" Freddy asked, grinning. The barber was in his late seventies and he loved to threaten his younger customers with a crew cut. "Save you a lot of money, you know? You wouldn't have to come back for six, maybe seven weeks."

"But I like seeing you, Freddy."

"Okay then." The barber turned off the razor and dropped it into a hand-tooled leather sheath that dangled from a black Lucite counter stocked with twenty-nine-cent combs and old bottles of activator fluid.

"How about half an inch all the way around?" Nash said.

"Above the ears on the sides?"

"Just a touch."

Even though Nash's hair was easy to cut—barbers had been telling him that ever since he was a kid—Freddy didn't rush to finish the job. He seemed glad for the company; it was a slow Monday afternoon.

"I noticed you seemed to be juggling a couple of young ladies at your apartment this weekend," the old man said as he gave Nash a once-over with the thinning scissors. "Not that it's any of my business."

"Are you married, Freddy?"

"For thirty-five years. Marlene passed on nearly ten years ago."

"I'm sorry."

Freddy carefully wiped down the thinning implement and picked up his long, steel clipping scissors.

"Did you ever have to choose between two women?" Nash asked.

"There was a time or two, yes," Freddy said. Nash looked into the wall mirror and saw the barber smiling. "About the only thing I remember about it is, it's best not to wait too long to make a decision. Otherwise, you're liable to lose 'em both."

"I'm glad to hear you say that."

"My advice costs nothing and it's worth it," Freddy said. "But if you don't mind one more friendly hint . . ."

"By all means."

"Once you do make up your mind, you can't have any regrets. You'll only be miserable if you do. Those regrets are liable to sour things with the one you keep, too. What's done is done. You remember that and you'll find happiness."

Nash stopped by his apartment before heading to the grocery store. He wanted to take a shower and wash all the itchy hairs off his back and shoulders. He also wanted to give Samantha a ring and tell her he was thinking about her.

He found a message from Jerry Povaric waiting for him. He'd spotted the transient named Virgil eating an early supper at a soup kitchen on Division Street. The cops had him in custody and would be calling Povaric as soon as they'd finished the interrogation. Both stories were coming together faster than Nash had imagined they would. Avery Graf would be pleased. Maybe Reg Devonshire would even be happy enough to discuss that raise he'd avoided at lunch last week.

He called Samantha and gave her the good news.

"I don't know if I can top all that tonight," she said. "But I'd sure like to give it a shot."

"What time should I come by?"

"About seven. And Nash?"

"Yes?"

"Bring a toothbrush."

Chapter Twenty-One

Early Tuesday afternoon, Nash and Povaric met Detective Josh Coltraine for lunch at a West Side pub called the Growler. When Nash was growing up, his father told him how his grandfather used to grab a pail of beer, called a growler, after he got off shift at the rendering plant. With the images of big jungle cats that *growler* conjured up in Nash's mind, it had become one of the magical words of his youth. Even now, the word seemed to pop into his head almost every time he had a beer.

They all started with a pint of Bass and the special of the house, a bowl of cheddar and beer soup. Nash and Povaric both ordered double cheeseburgers, loaded, but Coltraine only asked for fries.

"Hey, it's on us," Povaric said. "Have whatever you want."

"I'd like to, but my wife stuffed me full of German pancakes this morning. It's our twenty-fifth anniversary."

"Congratulations," Nash said.

"Thanks. If you don't mind, I'd like to make this kind of quick."

"Sure," Povaric said. "We understand."

Coltraine, a hale man of fifty, with thinning brown hair, had pinned-back ears and a faded scar over his left eye. He was saddled with a jazzman's last name and a pugilist's build. When he spoke in his soft baritone, his eyes narrowed into tiny slits.

"I don't have much to tell you, anyway," he said. "The suspect's named Virgil Hoops. He admits being in the parking garage the day Maynard Pike was killed. But he swears he didn't do it and he also swears he didn't see whoever did do it. Apparently, Virgil slept through the whole thing."

"Have you found the murder weapon?" Nash asked.

"Nope. Doubt if we ever will, either. It's pretty easy getting rid of a knife in a city this size."

"Did Hoops seem believable to you?"

"Not particularly. Unfortunately for our case, he volunteered to take a lie-detector test and passed. Either the guy's a total sociopath or he really didn't do it. I'd say it's about six one way, half dozen the other."

"Can you hold him?"

"Not for long. A, we don't have any physical evidence. No weapon, obviously, no latents on the body, and no blood on Virgil's clothes. B, no witnesses have come forward. And then there's the matter of the polygraph. Unless some new evidence pops up, we'll be turning him loose this afternoon."

"And here you are taking the day off," Povaric said.

Coltraine shrugged. "What can I do? Marge'll kill me if I don't take her shopping this afternoon and to the Tom Jones concert at the Vic tonight."

"Sounds like a blast."

"Ah, anniversaries are like weddings," the detective said. "They're for the wife."

"Let us know if you get any breaks," Nash said.

"Will do." Coltraine took a handful of fries and stood to leave.

"What time did you say you'd be letting Virgil Hoops off the hook?"

"Four o'clock." The detective took a swig of Bass for the road. "He's in a holding cell in the eighteenth precinct. If you want to talk to him, just tell the desk sergeant I sent you. By the way, thanks for lunch."

"Don't mention it," Povaric said as he dumped the rest of Coltraine's fries onto his plate.

They stopped by the newsroom to check for messages before going to see Virgil Hoops. While Povaric updated Phil Silvestri on his transportation stories, Nash made his way back to his desk.

The Fed-Ex package he found sitting there fairly bulged with possibilities. This might be the key to unlocking the Andrew Bond mystery, he thought as he opened the envelope from Curt Escobar. Inside he found an NCIC report marked "Confidential" and a brief note from his friend.

"Your instincts were right, as usual," Escobar began. *"But I think you're out of your depth on this one. The FBI is actively involved in this case. Watch your back, Rambler, and let me know how it all shakes out."*

The five-page dossier was quite revealing. The Russian's real name had been Andrei Kosarov. Picking Bond as an alias had been a cute touch.

Kosarov had been born in 1949, the only child of mid-level functionaries in the St. Petersburg cell of the Communist Party. After five years of service in the Soviet Army, he had resigned his commission of lieutenant colonel and transferred into the Moscow branch of the KGB. Kosarov fulfilled his assignments—which included rooting out and eliminating enemies of the state—so well that he earned a promotion to the KGB's London field office in 1987.

According to the dossier, Kosarov procured NATO defense secrets for the Soviets, but he'd also been known to straddle the fence once. Apparently, Kosarov made it known shortly after his arrival in London that he would sell information from his homeland to the highest bidder. Before the fall of Communism, he made seven trips back to Moscow and seven times he returned with a wealth of military and industrial secrets to peddle. He was such a shrewd wheeler-dealer that he became known in Western intelligence circles as The Hoarder.

Kosarov returned to Russia shortly after Yeltsin came to power. After that, the feds had lost track of him. Until last week.

Nash turned to the end of the report and scanned through the pertinent biographical information. As he read the last sentence, a chill ran down his back. When Andrei Kosarov killed those dissidents in Moscow, he had always used a knife.

Chapter Twenty-Two

"Let's construct a working hypothesis on this one," Povaric said as they drove to the eighteenth precinct to interview Virgil Hoops. Nash had filled his partner in on the Kosarov file on their way down to the old BMW.

"Okay," Nash said. "Let's say the two murders are connected somehow."

"Maybe this Kosarov guy is scared. One of his clients gets angry and threatens to kill him."

"I have Canfield Davis on tape telling his lawyer that most of Kosarov's information was out of date."

"There's your motive," Povaric said, smacking the dashboard with his right palm.

"Hey, watch it," Nash said. "This car is a classic."

"Classic candidate for the junkyard."

"I'll pretend I didn't hear that. Now if Davis got bad information, maybe Kosarov stiffed some of his other clients as well. I'm sure they wouldn't be happy about it, either."

"And it sounds like the FBI was hot on his trail, too."

"It's a cinch Kosarov felt jumpy as a cockroach on a hot plate."

"Nice image," Povaric said. "I'm still trying to digest my lunch here."

"What can I say, Jerry? This is not a job for the squeamish."

"All right. Kosarov's knocking off for the day, he's

walking through a dark, empty parking garage. Suddenly, Maynard Pike stumbles out of the shadows."

"Maybe Pike planned to mug him, maybe he wanted a handout."

"Maybe he just wanted to take a whiz."

"Whatever," Nash continued. "He steps out at the wrong time. Kosarov acts out of instinct and bam! He kills Pike with his handy dandy pig sticker."

"Then he runs. He's afraid there might be witnesses, so he decides now's as good a time as any to stuff the profits into his waistband and get on the next flight to Hollywood."

"Only he's got to wait until the banks open in the morning to close out his account."

"That's why he ends up at O'Hare the next day," Povaric said. "I like it."

"So who kills Kosarov?"

"Could be almost anybody. Canfield Davis, another angry customer. Maybe even some sort of Russian security force."

"But who gets off the shuttle train after the murder?"

"Nobody. Some homeless guy." Povaric slapped his leg. "Couldn't be, could it?"

Nash grinned. "I guess we'll just have to ask Virgil Hoops about that."

"Who'd you say referred you here?"

"Detective Coltraine."

They had been standing in line at the eighteenth precinct's front desk for forty-five minutes. The sergeant in charge of directing traffic in the station, an obese man with horribly clogged pores, was the best argument for early retirement Nash had ever seen.

"Hold on," the sergeant said, rubbing a pencil between

his neck wattles. "I'll check and see if he's in."

"Wait," Nash said as the man turned to check the duty roster hanging on the back wall. "We know he's not here. We didn't come to see Coltraine. He works out of Central."

The desk sergeant turned back slowly to face them. "Then why the hell are you asking for him?"

"We're not asking for him," Povaric said. "He told us to tell you he sent us to talk to one of his prisoners."

"Run that by me one more time."

"Let me try," Nash said. "We're here to talk to a man named Virgil Hoops. He's being held in your detention area. He's a suspect in a murder investigation. Detective Coltraine is in charge of that investigation. We're here from the *Daily Sentinel* and Coltraine said we could talk to Hoops before you release him this afternoon."

The sergeant nodded solemnly. "Well, why didn't you say so in the first place?"

While Nash waited for an officer to escort them in, Povaric went out the Chicago Avenue entrance to calm himself. After about five minutes, another cop, this one a young man with shocking red hair, emerged from the bowels of the precinct and called Nash's name.

"Right here," he replied.

"Are you the one looking to speak with Virgil Hoops?"

Nash nodded.

"I'm sorry, Mr. Hansen," the young cop said, "I'm afraid you're out of luck."

"What do you mean, out of luck?"

"We let Hoops go about half an hour ago."

"But Detective Coltraine said he was supposed to be held until four. It's only three-thirty right now."

"I know what time it is, sir," the young cop said. "It's true that we couldn't hold him any later than four, but that doesn't mean we had to keep him until the very last minute."

"The man is a suspect in a murder investigation. Why'd you let him out early?"

The cop cracked a funny looking smile. After a long pause, he said, "To tell you the truth, that man stunk like a shithouse in August."

Nash couldn't believe it. "You cut him loose because he smelled bad?"

"Look, the holding cell at this precinct sits right next to the bullpen area, where all the desks are. Nobody could get any work done all afternoon. I think he'd been crapping his drawers all day. I mean, I can't describe how bad this guy smelled. You could practically taste it. Not to mention the fact that he's uglier than a bagful of assholes. I'm telling you, if we hadn't let him go when we did, we would have had a full-scale police riot on our hands."

"For Christ's sake, you could have hosed him down or something."

"With all due respect, Mr. Hansen, if we pick that guy up again, I'll be sure to give you a call. Just remember to bring your sprinkler with you."

Chapter Twenty-Three

After two hours of searching, Nash and Povaric called it an afternoon. As he cruised back up Lake Shore Drive toward home, Nash tried to concentrate on the shimmering beauty of Lake Michigan to his right and the cool breeze circulating through the BMW. No matter what he tried, however, he couldn't get the frustration of losing Virgil Hoops out of his mind. They had been so close to possibly tying up both investigations. The situation was maddening.

Once he'd checked on Cyd and opened another stack of bills, Nash decided a warm, soothing shower was in order, followed by a large order of Hecky's rib tips and a couple bottles of ice cold Old Style for dinner. After that, he'd head straight for the sack. Unfortunately, Nash's plumbing decided not to cooperate with phase one of the operation. He ran the shower for five minutes, checking the temperature every few seconds with his finger, but the water stayed colder than the beer he planned to drink.

Disappointed, he turned off the shower and looked up his downstairs neighbor's phone number. Jake received a break on the rent every month by providing basic fix-it service to both apartments. At least he would be up now, enjoying his few hours of free time before the next White Castle graveyard shift.

"I don't know a thing about hot water heaters, Jake," Nash said. "I'm really sorry to bother you."

"Don't worry about it, pal. I'll get my tools and be up in five minutes."

Nash walked into the kitchen and opened the door to the water heater's alcove. The barrel of the shotgun he had borrowed from Slant Williams two weeks ago stared at him from the corner.

"Shit," he said, grabbing the weapon and cradling it carefully in his arms. Nash knew his old adviser would kill him if he had to miss even one of his coveted skeet shooting tournaments. Now seemed as good a time as any to make an apology.

"Don't shoot, it's only the plumber," Jake said. He carried a battered toolbox in his left hand and a flashlight in his right.

Nash pointed to the faulty heater. "Here's the patient. If you don't mind, I'm going to return this shotgun to a friend. I'll be right back."

"No problem," Jake said, grinning. "As long as you don't mind a few beers missing from your fridge when you come home."

Nash left his neighbor unpacking tools and drove the mile and a half to Slant Williams' house on the southeast side of Evanston, near the Chicago border.

"Ah, I never thought I'd see either of you again," Slant said when he opened the door. "You may be a First Amendment expert, Nash, but I'm afraid the Second doesn't guarantee you the right to keep and bear *my* arms."

"Sorry." Nash handed over the weapon. "Hope I didn't cost you any trophies."

Slant shook his head and beckoned Nash to follow him into the small, high-ceilinged bachelor apartment. "If I'd needed it, I would have called you. However, I must say it

146

was nice of you to bring it back of your own accord."

The Northwestern journalism professor stood on his small hide-a-bed couch and placed the shotgun back onto its polished oak display rack. "Makes me feel safer having her back watching over me, for some reason."

"Have you had dinner yet?"

"I was just getting ready to heat up a turkey pot pie. Care to join me?"

"How about a spinach stuffed pizza from Carmen's? My treat."

"I haven't had one of those in years," Slant said. "I seem to remember a remarkably buttery crust. And lots of cheese."

"That's the one."

"I'll have to postpone my next cholesterol test a couple of weeks, but what the hell. Let's live a little."

While they waited for the pizza to arrive, Nash brought Slant up to speed on the twists and turns of the investigations. The professor, in turn, recounted a few humorous examples of inter-office politics at Medill. After several minutes of these anecdotes, Slant pushed himself off the couch and walked over to the large bay window to watch the last embers of sunlight reflected off the lake.

"I'm thinking about retiring next year," he said, almost matter-of-factly.

Nash couldn't have been more surprised if Slant had revealed he was from Mars. He had been a professor for thirty-five years and, at fifty-seven, with no wife, no family, and very little in the way of a social life, teaching had become his *raison d'être*.

"Have you talked to the dean about this yet?"

"No. I'm still in the mulling-it-over stage. I'm trying to decide if I'm too old to be useful doing something else."

Nash joined his friend at the window and placed his palms on the spotless white sill. "What did you have in mind?"

"I've always loved geology, archaeology and anthropology," Slant said. "I've done quite a bit of reading in all three areas, even audited a few classes at Northwestern. It might be exciting to travel around, help out with some digs. See the world with a pickax and a pith helmet, you know?"

"Sounds great. You never know, I might even join you on a couple excavations."

"You think I should do it then?"

"This is the first time you've ever asked my advice."

Slant turned to him and smiled. "It's the first time I've thought you were mature enough to be of help."

"Gee, thanks."

"Seriously, though, I probably should begin planning for my future, what little of it I have left."

"I'm starting to have second thoughts about bringing back your shotgun, Slant."

"I remember you weren't in the highest of spirits the day you borrowed it."

Nash laughed at the vision of Elizabeth's gifts blasted all over the forest preserve. "It provided quite a cathartic release," he said.

"But we're avoiding the question at hand, aren't we?"

Nash paced the length of the threadbare rug. "Let me ask you this: Do you still feel wanted by the students and administrators?"

"I am quite at home in the department. And I don't see that changing any time soon."

"If you've still got something important to say in the classroom and you've got a comfortable place in which to say it, then maybe you shouldn't jump into this Indiana Jones thing feet-first."

"What do you suggest?"

"Why not take a sabbatical? See how you like hunting mummies for a year. The experience may rejuvenate your career."

"I'm certainly eligible for one. I just might check into the sabbatical option tomorrow at that." Just then, the doorbell rang, signaling the arrival of some of the best pizza anywhere.

"Thanks, Nash," Slant said as he buzzed in the deliveryman. "You've helped take a load off my shoulders."

"Don't look now, but this pizza's about to put one into your stomach."

"I can hardly wait."

On the drive home, Nash tried to imagine what it would be like to work in the same place for three-and-a-half decades. Unless the job involved a lot of luxury travel, he'd probably go crazy within five years. If everything worked out according to his admittedly vague career plans, he'd be writing books full-time, either non-fiction or novels, within ten years.

A thick plume of black smoke brought Nash back to the present as he turned onto his block. Hecky's didn't usually pump out this kind of volume. There were people and fire trucks everywhere. He followed the focus of activity until he came upon a sickening sight.

Although he couldn't quite bring himself to believe it, there was a smoking, smoldering pile of rubble right where his apartment used to be.

Chapter Twenty-Four

"Jake?" Nash called out as he wandered in a haze through the growing crowd. He recognized the faces of many of his other neighbors, curious and alarmed, but he did not see Jake's face among them.

"He's gone, boy." Freddy reached out and grabbed Nash's shoulder with a frail, shaking hand. "They pulled what was left of his body out of the rubble not five minutes ago."

A portable searchlight beam picked up the tears plotting a ragged course down Freddy's soot-stained cheeks; his face glistened like still water caught in the running lights of a boat. As the reality of the situation sank in, Nash began to feel the need for a handkerchief himself. Across the street, all the windows had been blown out of the storefronts, including Freddy's Barbershop. It must have been one hellacious blast. He picked his way through the mass of blackened wood and bricks, trying to find the cop in charge.

"I lived upstairs," Nash said to a man in blue barking out orders nearest the blast scene.

"You're damn lucky to be alive," said the man, a lieutenant in the Evanston police force. "Damn lucky."

"I heard you already pulled out a body."

The cop nodded. "That man was nearly cut in half by the explosion. He must have been right at the epicenter."

"He was my downstairs neighbor, Jake." As Nash began

telling him about the hot water heater, the cop signaled a forensics investigator to come over and listen.

"From the looks of things and what you're telling me, I'd say we're looking at a two-stage explosion," said the investigator, a woman named Joy Anderson.

"Do you think there was a bomb on the hot water heater?" Nash asked.

Anderson fixed him with a funny stare. "Son," she said, "that hot water heater *was* the bomb."

"I don't understand."

"It looks like somebody drained the water out of the heater and turned off the spigot so it stayed empty," Anderson said. "Then they must've cranked the heat up full blast."

"How would that create an explosion this size?" Judging by the puzzled look on the lieutenant's face, Nash wasn't the only one who was confused.

"When your neighbor opened up that spigot, there was an immediate, immense build-up of steam inside the heater. When the container filled up, in a split second, the excess steam made its own exit. The initial blast probably blew away the back third of the apartment, maybe even more, depending on the size of the heater."

"And Jake?"

"Killed instantly," Anderson said. "He never felt a thing."

"You mentioned two explosions," the lieutenant said.

"Yes. The second blast came from the ruptured gas line. Whoever set this thing up wasn't taking many chances with survivors."

"How can you be so sure the explosion was planned?" Nash asked.

Anderson called one of her technicians over to show

Nash a ten-foot stretch of yellow rubber tubing, the type used to drain waterbeds and hot water heaters. It had already been sealed inside an evidence bag.

"Whoever did this planned it to look like an accident," Anderson said. "But they got cocky and left their hose in the Dumpster around back. They must not have realized I don't get paid to write up an incident like this as an act of God. We take our work seriously up here."

Nash ran through the short list of suspects. Canfield Davis was an odds-on favorite for the job; he wanted to make sure his dealings with Kosarov didn't leak out. The same would also be true of Dr. Frederic Hintz. And then there was the long shot, Gil Francis. Although he blamed Nash for ruining his life, certainly motive enough for a killing, the ex–convention bureau president hardly seemed capable of a scheme this elaborate.

When Anderson went back to supervising the investigation, the lieutenant invited Nash over to a nearby fire truck to sit down and have a cup of coffee.

"I'd just as soon get you under wraps before the television crews show up," the officer said.

"What are you going to tell them?"

"We'll keep it as vague as possible tonight to give us a head-start on whoever did this." He scratched at the dark stubble on his chin. "We'll report one victim and say we haven't ruled out foul play."

"May I make a suggestion?" Nash asked.

"Shoot."

"It might be better to fudge a little bit on the body count, say something like you've found one body so far and you're still sifting through the rubble. Say you suspect there may be one other victim in there somewhere."

"You know the procedure pretty well."

"I write for the *Daily Sentinel*."

The officer laughed. "And you want us to lie to your fellow media types?"

"Let's just say I wouldn't mind if you fibbed a little on this one. Whoever set this bomb must've waited until my neighbor went to work last night before breaking into my place, and they obviously knew I was spending the night away from home." The cop's eyebrows raised on that one, but he kept his mouth shut and let Nash continue. "Which means they'd know we were both likely to be home at the time the explosion occurred."

"So if there's only one body, they might wonder if they got the right guy."

"I think you've got the general picture."

"You have a point. I'll play it like you said tonight, but I won't be able to keep a lid on this thing tomorrow."

Nash gave the officer his cell number, then used the phone to call Povaric and Samantha. Neither of them had heard about the blast, so the calls had upset rather than relieved them. He told them not to worry, and then made his way back to the rubble of his apartment to see if he could find anything worth saving.

He stumbled across a yellow aluminum softball bat near where his hall closet had been. The words "Ball Buster" emblazoned on the barrel were almost too smudged to read, but the bat remained intact. Nash couldn't say the same for the rest of his possessions. Unrecognizable hunks of melted plastic, wood and metal threw odd shadows onto the few still-standing sections of brick wall. Although he'd brought the tape of his interview with Canfield Davis into the newsroom for transcription, Andrei Kosarov's collection of photo CDs had melted into oblivion, one more missing link in the already-thin chain of evidence.

When he found the battered remains of the squirrel cage near where the front porch had been, Nash decided to stop exploring the wreckage. Cyd's lifeless form, impaled upon the twisted metal of his exercise wheel, was carnage enough for one night.

Chapter Twenty-Five

"If you're going to make a habit of staying over at Samantha's, you at least ought to remember to bring a change of clothes."

"Ha ha, Jerry."

Ever since he'd found out that both Canfield Davis and Dr. Hintz had been out of town when his water heater was sabotaged, Nash had been in what he believed to be an understandably foul mood. His partner, however, apparently would not rest until he was all cheered up.

"Come on, Nash, embrace the chaos." Povaric unwrapped a steaming-hot polish sausage and placed it on Nash's desk.

"What?"

"There's no sense dwelling on adversity. Use all that negative energy to create something new."

"I'm going to create a black eye for you if you don't shut up with that New Age malarkey."

"Sorry. It's from this book I've been reading on beating stress. My doctor tells me I'm a heart attack waiting to happen ever since the divorce, right?" Povaric paused to sample his pastrami on dark rye. "I just thought some calming words of wisdom might work for you, too."

Nash took a monster bite of sausage and washed it down with a swig of Dr Pepper.

"No, Jerry, this is the cure for what ails me." He held up

the rest of the wonderfully greasy dog. "And for that I thank you."

"There are many beers waiting for us on the outside. We can toast your fallen comrade into oblivion."

As the elevator doors closed behind them in the main lobby, Nash spotted Gil Francis coming through the revolving door about two hundred feet away.

"Oh shit," Nash said, pointing out the convention bureau chief.

Povaric whistled. "Looks like someone's moved way up on the list of bombing suspects."

"Stand directly between me and the main stairway, Jerry. If I walk straight back, maybe he won't see me."

"Too late," Povaric said as Francis broke into a trot toward them, his suit jacket draped over his right arm.

"Nash!" Francis yelled, gaining speed down the almost empty lobby.

"Get security," Nash said as he and Povaric both broke for the information desk at the foot of the *Sentinel*'s main staircase.

"Wait, Nash," Francis hollered. "I need to talk to you."

They made it to the desk twenty yards ahead of Francis. Povaric picked up the black security phone and said, "Lobby. Now. Possibly armed assailant."

"Stay back," Nash said to the fast-approaching Francis. "You don't want to do this." He grabbed a metal display rack from the info desk and swung it menacingly, spilling hundreds of brochures in a wide arc in front of him as the desk clerk ducked underneath the counter.

"Now hold on a minute," Francis said, pulling the jacket off his arm.

"Drop it, goddamnit," Nash ordered. Behind him, three

security guards ran down the steps with their guns drawn and ready.

Upon seeing all the firepower, Gil Francis stopped dead, gave Nash a bewildered look and dropped the fifth of Wild Turkey he'd been carrying onto the black-and-white tiled floor. At the sound of breaking glass, all three security guards cocked their revolvers.

"Don't even think about it," the lead officer said. "Get down on your knees with your hands behind your head. And I don't want to hear so much as a sneeze out of you."

While the security chief and another guard kept their guns trained on Francis, the third officer circled behind him, cuffed his hands behind his back and shoved him face-first into the floor.

"Whoa," Nash said.

The head of security holstered his gun and turned to face Nash. "And who the hell are you?"

"I'm the guy who thought he was being attacked," Nash replied. "But I think I just made a very big mistake."

"You bet your ass you did," Gil Francis said. He was back up on his knees again, and he looked mighty angry, especially with his bloody nose and cracked glasses.

"Look, you can uncuff him," Povaric said. "We fucked up."

"Yeah, we'll take it from here, fellas," Nash added. Outside, three squad cars full of Chicago's finest pulled to the curb. "And maybe you can tell the uniforms to go away, too."

"My union supervisor's going to hear about this one," the head guard said as he motioned his two underlings to go meet the cops.

"And do you think you could unlock the cuffs, please?" Povaric asked. It was as gentle a request as Nash had ever heard him make.

After all the law enforcement had cleared out of the lobby, Nash and Povaric led Francis to the lobby restroom.

"I'm really sorry, Gil," Nash said while Francis mopped the blood off his chin with a wet paper towel. "Someone torched my apartment last night and I've been a little jumpy because of it."

"Doesn't excuse the kind of bullshit abuse I was subjected to out there," Francis grunted.

"You did threaten him a few days ago," Povaric said.

"You're fucking-a right I did. I thought the goddamn punk had cost me my career."

"You mean you're still head of the bureau?" Nash asked.

"Yeah. The board refused to accept my resignation." Francis readjusted his tie and threw his glasses into the nearest trashcan. "They recognized the fact that I busted my balls to keep the electronics expo in town and they know they couldn't find anyone better for this crappy job."

"That's great news, Gil. I'm sorry I was so quick to think badly of you."

"And here I am trying to apologize for what I did with a bottle of your favorite booze."

Nash glanced at their reflections in the mirror. They all looked like shit—Francis with his bloody nose, Nash with his second-day outfit and Povaric on his usual high-stress alert. He had to laugh at the picture.

"I suppose that's the best way to handle this fiasco," Francis said. "Laugh it off and forget it. The way I figure it, we're about even now."

He held out his hand and Nash shook it, gladly.

"I'll call you in a few weeks," Nash said. "After you've had a chance to lick your wounds."

"Don't press your luck," Francis said. "Better make it a month."

Nash decided to skip the drinks and attend to the unfortunate chore of updating Reg Devonshire on the non-progress of both murder investigations. He found the managing editor ensconced in his small office just off the newsroom floor, poring over reporter expense-account submissions before rejecting them or passing them on to accounting for reimbursement. The reject pile was twice as high as the approval stack.

"Come in, Nash," Devonshire said without looking up.

"I'd hate to interrupt you while you're supporting the troops."

The editor cocked his head at Nash as if trying to figure out a piece of abstract art. "I understand that my style is not your style," he said. "Further, I understand that you dislike me. But just because I run a tight, highly ethical, family-friendly journalistic ship, that does not mean I give an iota less than my full support to the entire editorial staff. Including you."

"My wisecrack was out of line," Nash said as he eased into the visitor's chair. "I've had a very bad, extremely exhausting day."

"A trained journalist using two adverbs in the same sentence—you must be tired."

Nash was ready to shoot off his mouth again, until he realized Devonshire was smiling. It seemed to be his idea of a joke.

"I heard about your apartment," the editor added. "I'm sorry."

"Thanks Reg. I appreciate it."

"The police suspect arson?"

"The investigator seemed pretty certain."

"Could it have anything to do with the stories you're working on?"

If Nash told Devonshire what he suspected, it might prompt the editor to assign the stories to someone else. It also would open the door to an uncomfortable examination of his reporting methods. "I'm not sure," he offered.

"Don't worry, Nash. I'm not pulling you off the case. But I can give you an extra body or two for legwork, if needed."

"Thanks. I'll keep that offer in my back pocket."

"Okay. Just one more thing." The editor looked over Nash's shoulder, as if making sure no one was passing within earshot.

"What is it, Reg?"

"Deserved or not, you have a reputation for bending the rules if they hinder your pursuit of a good story. That's why I've been so chilly toward you. I don't care about your silly anti-authority attitude."

"Glad to hear it."

"I'm not finished." Devonshire placed both hands flat on his desk and leaned forward. "With your training, you don't require an ethics lecture about why the ends don't justify the means when you're upholding a public trust. But someone apparently tried to kill you last night, which gives me reason to suspect that you've hit a nerve with some very bad people. As a result, your neighbor was killed and the profile of this investigation has gone through the roof. So I'm warning you, Nash: If you're coloring outside the lines, you'll not only be out of a job but I'll make it my personal mission to make sure you're kicked so far out of the profession you won't even be able to get a newspaper subscription."

Nash gave Devonshire a sharp nod and said, "You're getting more likable every day, Reg."

Besides arranging for his mail to be held for him at the Evanston Post Office, Nash was too busy brooding to do any useful work for the rest of the afternoon. By six, he felt almost too tired to make it back over to Samantha's. But the thought of her gentle touch and the soft sheets on her bed provided impetus enough to get him into the car and over to River North in record time.

"I've got a surprise for you," Sam said when Nash plopped onto her couch.

"Can I enjoy it from here?" he asked.

"You most certainly can, sleepy boy." She disappeared into the bedroom for a moment and returned with an armful of bags and boxes from Field's, Nordstrom's, Bloomingdale's—the best department stores in town.

"I hope the clothes you have on fit you well," Samantha said as she dropped the packages in a pile at his feet. "Because I peeked at the tags while you were in the shower to get your measurements."

"This is too much." Nash leaned back against the cushions, overwhelmed by her generosity.

"Nonsense. I've always wanted to select a whole new wardrobe for a man. And now you've given me my big chance to do a total make-over."

"Like 'Queer Eye for the Straight Guy'? I hope you're not going to ruin my image."

"I'm afraid Goodwill wouldn't take any of my credit cards, so you're going to have to live with being a bit more . . . sartorial."

"They sure teach big words in veterinary school."

When she smiled, he stood up and kissed her, holding

161

her in his arms for a long minute. "Thanks for cheering me up. Jerry tried all day, but I'm afraid he doesn't quite have the knack."

"He doesn't have anything like these, either," she said, pulling back and unbuttoning the top three buttons on her blouse.

"Well, yes he does," Nash said, leaning over to kiss her exposed collarbone. "They just aren't as shapely."

"Hold on there a minute, sailor." Samantha pushed Nash onto the couch. "No more kisses until I see you dressed up in some of these fancy new duds."

"Aye, aye, skipper."

Chapter Twenty-Six

At 3:17 a.m., Nash awoke to a rustling sound. It appeared to be coming from the living room.

"Samantha," he whispered. "Did you leave the window open?"

"I don't think so," she murmured, more asleep than awake.

"Is there a gun in the house?" he asked, more insistent. At that, Samantha's eyes froze open. Nash put his index finger to her lips.

"A gun. Do you own a gun?"

She nodded slowly, and he could see the terror welling up in her eyes. He felt pretty uneasy himself.

"It's in the bottom drawer of my filing cabinet," she whispered, pointing to the far side of the room. "Bullets are in a box next to it. My mom gave it to me when I moved out of the house. It's never been fired."

Nash eased out of bed and walked gingerly across the room. As he opened the door of the filing cabinet, he heard a dull thud from the living room. He fumbled with the small automatic handgun, undoing the catch and releasing the five-shot magazine into his palm. He had inserted three bullets when he heard another thud.

Motioning for Samantha to get down next to the bed, Nash slapped the magazine home, clicked off the safety and slipped the gun behind his back and into the tight elastic band of his new underwear. When a flashlight beam swept under the door, Nash took a deep breath, grabbed the yellow softball bat propped against the dresser and stepped into the living room.

He was startled by a flood of light as someone turned on the florescent lamp hanging from the ceiling.

"Looks like we've got the right place," said the man at the switch. To his right, near the window overlooking the fire escape, stood another, larger man. He giggled at the sight of Nash brandishing a bat in his skivvies.

"It's Jim fucking Palmer," the giggler said.

"Palmer was a pitcher, asshole," Nash said as he advanced toward the man. "Who the hell are you?"

Giggler stopped smiling and opened his trench coat. From a long shoulder holster, he pulled out a shotgun with a pistol grip.

"What the fuck is that?" Nash asked.

"Your ticket off the planet if you don't drop that bat and start cooperating," the man at the light switch said. He made no move to draw a gun of his own, but Nash assumed everyone in the room was armed. Still, Giggler presented the most immediate threat.

"Why not just kill me right here?" Nash asked.

"Yeah," Giggler said, giving Light Switch a lopsided grin. "Why don't we waste him right now?"

"I'd rather do this someplace with a little more privacy, Mr. Hansen," Light Switch said. "But if you'd prefer to end it all here, we'll be happy to accommodate."

"I've already dialed nine-one-one."

"Pretty good trick with the phone line cut and both cell phones sitting in those chargers on the breakfast bar," Light Switch said. "Now drop the fucking bat before we turn you into guacamole."

"Sounds fair to me," Nash said. He turned toward Giggler and heaved the bat in his direction. When the big man jumped out of the way, Nash reached around to the back of his underwear, grabbed the little automatic and drilled three holes in Giggler's chest.

"Who brought the chips?" Nash said as he turned the gun on Giggler's partner. "You can't eat guacamole without chips, can you, asshole?"

Light Switch made a move for his jacket pocket, but Nash pulled the hammer back on the pistol and shook his head. Even though he was now out of bullets, it was an effective move.

"You can come out now, Samantha," Nash said, keeping his eyes and the gun trained on Light Switch. "I could use a little assistance here."

She emerged from the bedroom visibly shaking, her long peach nightgown swishing against her legs.

"Honey, it's okay," Nash said. "Pick up that bat and bring it to me. And you, Mr. Party Crasher, you get down on your knees and put your hands behind your head." He'd learned something from the Gil Francis episode after all.

When Light Switch was in position, Nash handed Samantha the unloaded gun and had her train it on the kneeling man.

"Where's your piece?"

"Right pocket of the windbreaker," the man said.

Nash walked behind the intruder and fished the gun out with two fingers of his left hand. It was a .22 target pistol.

"What are you, fucking hitmen?" Nash asked, stepping back and pointing the gun at the man's head.

"Yeah, we're wise guys," Light Switch said. His voice sounded somehow familiar.

"I don't like your attitude, wise guy." Nash stepped forward and gave the man a one-handed smack on the shoulder with the aluminum bat. He heard sirens down the street and realized he didn't have much time to find out what he needed to know.

"Sam, go outside and tell the cops where we are and what's going on," Nash said as he prodded the man up onto the couch.

"She's a fucking dead woman," Light Switch snarled. "Just like you're going to be dead. Soon as word of this gets out, you won't have any place to hide."

"As soon as word gets out to whom?" Nash asked, cocking the little .22.

"The mob. Who do you think?"

"Cut the crap. There's no reason for the mob to be after me. Who the fuck do you work for? Don't think I won't shoot you if you don't tell me. Look at your friend over there."

"Go ahead and shoot then, because I'm not telling you shit."

"Loyal son of a bitch, aren't you." Suddenly, Nash knew where he'd heard the voice before. "You're Canfield Davis' receptionist."

"Never heard of him," the man said. "And I know he's never heard of me."

Before the first policeman made it to Samantha's door, Nash gave old Light Switch the concussion of a lifetime. He hoped that by taking two of Canfield Davis' men out of commission—one permanently—he would put the defense contractor on the defensive. Davis wouldn't scare easily, but Nash imagined this message might be strong enough to keep him from launching a full frontal assault, at least for a while.

★ ★ ★ ★ ★

As he and Samantha watched a team of paramedics wheel the two thugs out on collapsible gurneys, Nash felt numb and queasy. It was the same reaction he'd had two years ago in San Bernardino after he'd gunned down a survivalist preacher named Reese Stevens and Klete Patterson, a renegade cop. Nash wondered if he could ever get used to this kind of killing. He hoped he would never find out.

Chapter Twenty-Seven

Attending the funeral of a man who was murdered because he had strayed too close to one of his investigations dredged up even more familiar, horrible feelings in Nash. Maybe Jake wouldn't be missed down at the White Castle, but judging by the large crowd at the Evanston funeral parlor Thursday morning, Nash's neighbor had left behind more than his share of friends to grieve for him.

He only stayed long enough to pay his respects to Jake's parents, but he left the funeral home with a renewed sense of resolve; he would bring Canfield Davis down even if he had to do it alone. And judging by the way Davis covered his tracks, it just might come down to that, Nash thought as he headed downtown to give a full statement on last night's confrontation to a Chicago homicide detective.

Davis had jumped on the first Lear jet to Washington after their conversation Monday afternoon, just in time to get himself an alibi for the apartment bombing and Nash's murder—if all had gone as expected. According to the cop he'd talked to at 8:30, Davis was expected back in the area Friday afternoon. Nash planned to be on hand to greet him.

First, though, he had to get down to Central Station at 12th and State to give a complete deposition. He hoped the city attorney's office wouldn't get a wild hair and decide to bring him up on a murder charge.

After waiting half an hour in a drab interrogation room

with Lorenzo Nugent, the *Sentinel*'s attorney, Nash heard a short, sharp rap on the door. He was pleased to see Detective Josh Coltraine had been assigned to the case.

"Nash, good to see you again," Coltraine said. He gave Nugent a nod and eased into a low-back chair on the other side of the gray metal table.

"You know each other?" Nugent asked.

"Jerry Povaric and I discussed the murder of the homeless man at McCormick Place with Detective Coltraine on Monday. They had a suspect in custody, since released."

"On behalf of the Chicago Police Department, I apologize for letting Virgil Hoops go early. If I'd been in the office that day . . ."

"We might have solved the Andrew Bond killing. And maybe the Maynard Pike case, too."

"We're still looking for Hoops, Nash. If we found him once, we'll find him again."

"Hate to remind you, Detective, but Povaric spotted Hoops and called your guys in."

"And how is your partner doing these days?"

"Pissed off that he has to go track down Hoops again."

"I hope he's not angry enough to do something stupid, like forget to phone us if he runs across a suspect in a capital case."

"No, Coltraine, we journalists are the smart ones, remember?"

The detective leaned across the table and breathed stale cigarette breath into Nash's face. "Keep it up and I might forget to recommend a finding of justifiable homicide for your little vigilante act last night."

"You sound a lot like a man who just had a shitty wedding anniversary," Nash said, leaning forward until their noses were almost touching. "Now, are we going to cut the crap and get down to business or do I have to solve these fucking cases all by myself?"

"Don't push it, Nash," Coltraine said. "I'm the one asking the questions today."

Lorenzo Nugent, used to arguing open-meetings cases and taking depositions in libel disputes, had turned a very light shade of pale during the exchange.

"Nash, I'd advise you not to volunteer any further statements," he stammered.

"It's okay, Lorenzo. Could you give us a moment to work this out?"

"It's highly irregular to excuse one's counsel in the middle of an interrogation," Nugent said.

"Trust me," Nash said as Coltraine opened the door. "This is a highly irregular interrogation."

After Nugent had gone, Coltraine poured them both a cup of coffee and loosened his tie. "You were right about the anniversary, by the way," he said. "Two hours of Tom fucking Jones. And to celebrate twenty-five years of marriage, Marge balls up a pair of silk French-cut panties and throws them on stage right in front of God and everybody. It was humiliating."

Nash grinned. "I bet the sex was great afterward."

"For her, sure. But it's hard to get into the act when your partner is looking into your face and picturing a certain over-the-hill Welshman with a giant package."

"I can see where that might be a problem."

"Yeah, but what can you do?" Coltraine shrugged. "So why don't you cut a poor married guy some slack and tell me what you've turned up."

Nash pulled a microcassette out of his shirt pocket and slid it across the table. "That's a copy of a conversation I had with Canfield Davis Monday afternoon. The next day, my apartment blew up. Yesterday, he sent two goons around my girlfriend's house to kill me."

"The Evanston cops haven't been able to trace the bombing to Davis, or anybody else for that matter. And there's no record of either of your assailants in the personnel files of Midwest Avionics. Add that to the fact Davis was out of town on the days in question, and I'm afraid a simple phone threat—most likely recorded without your subject's consent—doesn't amount to shit."

"The secretary's voice is on there, too," Nash said. "You'll find it matches the dulcet tones of my attacker."

"Which one?"

"The living one."

"Gee, that's lucky."

"Are you going to check it out or not?"

"Sure, Nash. But again, if you recorded without consent, it's inadmissible."

"It might give you some leverage on Davis when he comes back."

"I doubt it." Coltraine lit a cigarette. "I'd be willing to bet Davis' attorney is camped out on the tarmac right now waiting for his client's return."

"Have you got names for the attackers yet?"

"I prefer Pebbles and Bam-Bam myself."

"I'll take that as a no."

"Then you take it wrong. The dead man's nickname was Tony Knuckles."

"Freelance assassin?"

"How'd you guess?"

"And what about Davis' Boy Friday?"

"Alleged Boy Friday."

"Right."

Coltraine pulled a black-and-white mug shot out of his

171

inside coat pocket and laid it on the table. "Meet Hank Spielman, the man you sent to the hospital. Nailed on a breaking-and-entering rap in a Mundelein office park twelve years ago."

"Did he ever do time?"

"Nope. Six months, suspended. And his jacket's been clean ever since."

"He was probably engaging in some good old industrial espionage."

Coltraine shrugged. "Who's to say?"

"You want to check up on it?"

"Any other requests?"

"Only one. Find out if Spielman served in the military, and if he ever crossed Davis' path during his tour."

"And what are you going to do to earn your salary this week?" Coltraine asked.

"I'm just going to try and stay alive."

Chapter Twenty-Eight

Nash made it back to Samantha's by 7:00, no closer to cracking the story than he had been in the interrogation room that morning. Sam had left a message on her answering machine telling him she was tied up in emergency surgery and didn't know when she'd be home.

He threw on a light windbreaker—one of the numerous items Samantha had picked out for him—and wandered around the neighborhood for about an hour. Along the way he picked up a fifth of Wild Turkey, a few magazines, some baguettes and all the fixings for a huge Greek salad. Almost as an afterthought, he grabbed a bottle of carpet cleaner to get rid of the patch of blood Tony Knuckles had so rudely leaked onto the floor of Sam's apartment when he died.

Nash sprayed a mountain of foamy cleaner onto the dark brown stain. At least he wouldn't have to re-plaster the wall; the small-caliber bullets from Samantha's gun had entered the massive frame of Tony Knuckles just fine, but none of them had managed to make their way out the other side. Kind of like a roach motel.

When Sam finally arrived at 9:15, he was adding the finishing touches—grated feta, huge Greek olives—to the salad and watching the last few innings of a Cubs away game on the small color TV hanging under one of the kitchen cabinets.

"Soup's on," Nash called into the living room.

She dropped her purse on the floor as she crossed the threshold into the kitchen and walked up to hug him from behind.

"We've got to get you in here more often, boy," she said, popping an olive into her mouth. "This is a little chunky for soup."

"How did the operation go?"

"A beautiful German Shepherd got hit by a car, lots of internal bleeding." She laid her head on Nash's shoulder. "I really thought I could save him. But after two hours, he was still so full of blood. It was like trying to sew up Swiss cheese. We had to put him down."

He turned around and put his hands on her shoulders. "That's rough, sweetheart."

She sniffled and pulled his arms down around her so that his hands overlapped on the small of her back.

"I can't imagine working in a profession where you have to deal with that kind of loss every day," he said.

"It's happy work at least half the time. And I don't usually get this upset over losing an animal anymore. You have to realize you can't save every life and then focus your thoughts on the ones you can help."

"Sounds like a healthy attitude."

"Once in a while, though, it hits you. Especially with the dogs. They're so noble and unsophisticated at the same time. They don't have any idea why they're in so much pain, they can't comprehend it. Yet you can see they're trying not to cry, trying not to let you know how much it hurts. It breaks my heart, Nash."

There was a heavy moment of silence, and then she let it all loose. The horror and sadness of the surgery and the killing in her apartment the night before, all of it came tumbling out in a torrent of tears. Nash led her back into the living room, walking her backwards, her face still buried in his chest. The sobbing broke once on the way, when she stumbled over her purse and nearly landed them both on the floor. Startled, she had caught her breath for a moment, but otherwise, Samantha cried without respite for nearly ten minutes.

Nash held her on the couch and smoothed back her hair the way he would a child's. He didn't talk so much as repeat the same soothing sounds over and over, kissing her damp forehead whenever she came up for a few gulps of air.

She calmed down in stages, first hiccupping, then offering up embarrassed apologies as she blotted her face with tissues. Finally, she shuddered with exhaustion and Nash could feel the tension slipping from her muscles as she closed her eyes and fell asleep curled up next to him, her head on his lap. Although his legs soon began falling asleep and he couldn't lean back without pinching his neck, Nash let her stay right where she was, afraid the slightest movement would wake her and send her off on another jag.

He came to with a start when Samantha kicked him in the head. It was midnight and Nash lay on his side, his head facing the window. Samantha had passed out in front of him on the couch, her head toward the door and her bare feet resting just below his chin. She kicked him in the cheek when she'd started slipping onto the floor, and the motion awakened them both.

"Sorry, baby," she murmured. She sprawled between the couch and the coffee table, rubbing at her eyes with the palms of her hands. Nash leaned over to help her into a sitting position.

"You feel better?" he asked.

"Drained. And hungry. Do you think the salad's still all right?"

"Should be."

They ate in the small dining nook off the kitchen, forking big chunks of salad straight out of the bowl. He uncapped the bourbon and poured four fingers over a generous helping of ice; she drank mineral water with lemon. They both agreed the salad was perfect.

"Do you want to talk about it?" he asked as he got up to pour himself a second, lighter drink.

"Talk about what?"

"Whatever's got you so upset?"

"I already told you."

"Part of it, maybe."

She joined him at the counter, grabbed a cup off a wall hook and gave his left shoulder a gentle squeeze. But from the pained look on Samantha's face, Nash could tell there were things besides coffee mugs hanging in the air.

"I think I'll join you for a drink," she said.

"With water?" he asked, holding up the bottle of Turkey.

"On the rocks will be fine."

"My favorite mixer." He grabbed a tray of cubes from the freezer, wondering how to get her to open up. He knew he should proceed carefully.

"When exactly did you switch from med school to veterinary medicine?" he asked.

"Two weeks before we were scheduled to do our first cadaver work."

"Uh huh. And you've managed to avoid seeing dead bodies up close ever since."

"Until last night."

"That's what I thought." He handed her the drink and

took a long pull on his own. Although he'd never smoked, he felt a strong urge to light up a cigarette and fill his lungs with nicotine. Anything to calm his nerves.

"Was last night the first time for you?" she asked.

"No. I've seen dead bodies before."

"I meant, was it the first time you'd ever made one?"

He shook his head. "It seems to have become something of a habit with me."

She shuddered and took another drink.

"I probably mess around in other people's business more often than most reporters," he continued. "It's sometimes nasty business and people don't appreciate having it exposed. That usually sets some kind of violence into motion—violence involving me and sometimes the people close to me."

"You could quit," she said quietly.

"Yes. But I'm not going to."

"Why?"

He shrugged. "I'm a good reporter. It's the only thing I know how to be. And to keep being a good reporter, I can't look the other way whenever a dangerous story comes along. I don't purposefully seek out these situations, but I can't let people get away with murder if I have a chance to stop them."

"How can you kill another person?"

He wanted to take her in his arms, but settled for another shot of bourbon instead. What was he supposed to do, just let those thugs kill him, and probably Samantha as well? Still, he could see her point. Repeatedly killing your fellow humans—even when they were trying to kill you first—wasn't exactly considered normal conduct. And although the killing never made him feel good, he didn't have any nightmares about it, either.

"I care about you, Samantha. I was trying to protect you."

She shook her head violently. "No. Don't try to put that on me, Nash. I could tell when I came into the room that you would have pulled the trigger whether I was in the apartment or not. You ordered me and that man around like an angry god addressing his creations. I never imagined you like that. So . . . frightening."

"I didn't realize I scared you. I was just trying to keep the situation under control and get us both out of there alive. I'm sure the adrenaline was pumping at a pretty high rate, but . . ."

"I don't know, Nash. Maybe my reaction to last night just proves we're going too fast. I mean, what do we really know about each other? That we're good together in bed? That we make each other laugh? We don't even know each other's birthdays and here we are living together."

"I'm sorry my apartment blew up, Sam. If I'd known you felt uneasy, I would have asked Canfield Davis to put it off for a week or two."

"That's not what I meant, Nash. If we're going to fight, you could at least try and fight fair."

He walked over to her and put his arms out. "You're right. I'm sorry."

"Me too, lover," she said, accepting his embrace. "I'm just not used to all this craziness."

"I've put you through a lot."

She looked up at him and nodded. "I need some time to catch my breath if we're going to make this relationship work."

"So you think we still can?"

"I don't know. But after what we've gone through this week, maybe anything's possible."

178

He felt one of the many knots in his stomach begin to loosen when she smiled. Unfortunately, there were still enough ropes tied up in there to qualify him for a merit badge.

Chapter Twenty-Nine

They agreed Nash would find another place to stay the next day, at least until he and Samantha got to know each other better. So he arrived at the *Sentinel* Friday morning with little more than a bundle of new clothes, half a bottle of whiskey and a tarnished softball bat to his name—and nowhere besides the trunk of the old BMW to put any of it.

Even though he felt about as low as he could get, Nash knew when he saw Jerry Povaric's face that his partner probably felt lower. Povaric's right eye was clouded with blood, his left ear was heavily bandaged and the rest of his face was a mass of cuts and bruises. In addition, his left arm was in a sling, and when he got up to talk to Nash, he walked with a noticeable limp.

Nash let out a deep breath. "I guess since you're the transportation reporter, I should ask if you got the plate number of the truck that ran over you."

"Yeah. It read H-O-O-P-S."

"Holy shit, Virgil did this to you?"

Povaric eased a cheek onto Nash's desk. "None other than."

"Did the cops get him?"

"Nah, I didn't want to call those fuck-ups in until I got some answers. You know, I figured I'm this big tough guy who'd have no problem mopping up the floor with a broken-down transient like Hoops."

"Did you find out anything before he . . ."

"Before he what? Pulverized me? Clobbered me?" Povaric swept a stack of papers onto the floor. "I feel like a freaking idiot, Nash. And no, I didn't find out anything except that Virgil Hoops is one crazy son of a bitch. And he stinks just as bad as those cops said he did."

"Where'd you find him?"

"I went back to that soup kitchen on Division and asked around. Some old woman told me Hoops holed up in an abandoned warehouse on King Drive. I went over there and found him sitting in a park about a block away, feeding the goddamn pigeons. I thought, jeez, this guy must not be as tough as everyone makes him out to be." Povaric shook his head. "I just checked out of Northwestern Memorial a few hours ago."

"What do you want to do?"

"I want to kill that asshole. Why'd you send me out looking for him again yesterday anyway? Why'd you get to go schmooze Coltraine down at Central for a few hours while I'm out looking under rocks and nearly getting myself killed? Why the hell is a punk twenty-five-year-old business writer running this investigation in the first place, huh?"

Povaric was yelling now, and all activity around him had ground to a halt. So much for open newsrooms. Nash made a note to make sure the next paper he worked on gave beat reporters their own cubicles.

"Jerry, I truly wish you hadn't gotten the shit kicked out of you yesterday. But I want you to remember I've been out on the street almost as much as you. My fucking apartment got blown up this week and two guys with guns tried to kill me, okay? And the only reason I sent you out after Hoops is that I know you get bored when there's no action."

"The hell with all that, man. I don't know why I let you

rope me into this bullshit. But from now on, I am through with this investigation and I am through with you."

"I'm sorry to hear that, Jerry, because Samantha just threw me out of her apartment. And I was hoping to stay at your place for a while."

At that, the rage seemed to drain right out of Povaric's face. He sat back down on Nash's desk and rubbed his forehead.

"Aw, Christ," he said. "You should have told me sooner. What kind of guy would let a friend run on and make a fool of himself like that?" Povaric looked around the newsroom and rolled his eyes at all the attention he was getting.

"Read about it in tomorrow's *Sentinel*," he hollered as the other reporters went back to work. "So what do you say, care to crash on my couch for a couple of days?" Povaric extended his good hand and Nash gripped it.

"I'm sorry if I've been ordering you around," Nash said.

"Nah. It's just kind of an adjustment, putting my trust in a mere infant such as yourself. I'm sure I'll get used to it in time."

"So, how do you think we should proceed?"

Povaric nodded his head toward Reg Devonshire, who was fast approaching the desk. "Why don't we ask him?"

"I think it's about time we conferenced with Mr. Graf," the managing editor said when he arrived. "It appears your investigation has hit some rocky shoals, and I'm growing weary of throwing away this paper's time, money and reputation on a story that may never be written."

Avery Graf was on the phone when his secretary ushered the three of them into his office, and he motioned for them to sit. The publisher's office, several floors above the newsroom, commanded almost as much respect as the man who used it. He had a large suite, with an adjoining private bathroom and small conference room, all to himself. The floor of the main chamber was black marble and the walls were tiled with highly burnished rose quartz. Low track lighting and several works of modern art on the side walls added some warmth to the room, as did a view of Navy Pier similar to the one Nash and Povaric had enjoyed on occasion in the meeting room upstairs.

The three visitors sat in the center of the office on antique overstuffed chairs that rested on a magnificent Oriental rug. The carpet extended under Graf's desk, a dark oak number with clawed feet and a glass top. The surface of the desk was clear save for a portable phone base and a leather-bound appointment calendar. It was the kind of place where guests waited quietly.

After a few minutes, Povaric nudged Nash's arm. "I forgot to ask you," he whispered. "Does she have a middle name?"

"Who?" Nash mouthed. Devonshire fixed them with a nasty glare, but Graf didn't seem to notice that anyone else in the room was talking.

"Samantha Parker," Povaric said.

"No. Not yet, anyway."

Povaric nodded approvingly. "I'll keep my fingers crossed."

"Thanks."

When Graf hung up a few minutes later, he apologized for the wait and offered coffee all around.

"When the governor calls, I'm afraid you must always answer the phone." Graf sat back down and poured a trace of cream into his cup. "But now, to important matters. Nash, it's been ten days since you began investigating the murder of Maynard Pike. As I understand it from Reg, that investigation has expanded to include the killing of a former KGB spy who may have stabbed Pike. As a direct result of your efforts, you and Jerry Povaric have written three small updates on the crimes. Also, your apartment building was blown up with your neighbor in it. And until I spoke with him this morning, the DA was thinking about charging you with manslaughter for gunning down an intruder in a young woman's apartment early Thursday morning. Did I leave anything out?"

"That's pretty much the size of it, Avery," Nash replied. He looked over at Povaric, who shifted in his seat.

"I'm concerned that the longer they stay on this story, the messier it seems to be getting," Devonshire chimed in.

Graf waved the managing editor off and took a sip of coffee. "I knew the case wouldn't be cracked overnight when I assigned it to them, Reg. But now is the time to assess the situation and decide how to proceed."

"It's time and money down the drain if you pull the plug on us now," Povaric offered. He leaned forward to avoid eye contact with Devonshire.

"That may be true," Graf said. "But if we still don't have the story ten days down the road . . ."

"What do you need to know?" Nash asked.

"Two things: First, is this becoming too dangerous for you to handle?"

Glancing at the bruises on Povaric's face, Nash was tempted to answer in the affirmative, but Povaric stared him down.

"I think we're on the downhill side of the story, at least as far as violence is concerned," Nash said.

"Couldn't get much worse, anyway," Povaric added.

Graf smiled and said, "Question two: Can you break this story?"

Nash and Povaric both nodded vigorously.

Devonshire shook his just as hard. "We can't indefinitely extend this investigation on a hunch," he said. "We must at least set a deadline."

"At this point, Reg, I'm inclined to agree," Graf said. "Were you two planning to work over the weekend?"

"I'm not planning to stop until I've got the story, whether I'm back on my beat or not," Nash said.

"Me either," Povaric added.

"I hope it doesn't come to that," Graf said. "But I certainly admire your tenacity. Let's meet again Monday morning and discuss results."

"That doesn't give us much time," Nash said.

"No, it doesn't," the publisher replied.

Apparently, it was all the time they were going to get.

Chapter Thirty

"At least neither of us has any dates to cancel this weekend," Povaric said as he tried to work the cap off a bottle of ibuprofen.

Nash reached across the desk and said, "Let me help you with that."

"Nah, it's supposed to be childproof."

Nash gave him the finger as Povaric yanked the lid off with his teeth, sending an arc of little yellow pills flying over his shoulder.

"Son of a bitch," Povaric said. He tried to lean over and pick up the two nearest tablets, but fell off his chair instead. "Goddamn this bum leg. Lost my balance."

Nash couldn't help laughing, but he had the decency to swivel around so Povaric wouldn't see him.

"I hear that, you bastard," Povaric said, hoisting himself back into his seat. "I'll be damned if this isn't one of the worst weeks of my life."

"Are you that pissed?"

"I've never lost a fight before, and I wasn't hoping to break the streak by underestimating some rummy old bum."

"You'll get over it."

"Yeah, but if I ever find Virgil Hoops again, he won't."

Nash picked up the phone, dialed the homicide division and asked for Detective Coltraine's extension.

"What," a gruff voice said.

"Your mother teach you any manners, Coltraine?"

"Let's just leave my mama out of this, Hansen. What the hell do you want?"

"Why the foul mood?"

"My wife just called. Seems Tom Jones has been held over and Marge will just die if we don't go."

"Make her go with a girlfriend."

"Can't. I told her he was my favorite singer, too."

"You did what?"

"I wanted to make her happy on our anniversary, Nash. She wouldn't have enjoyed the concert half as much if she knew I'd gone because I had to."

"You're insane, Coltraine."

"Yeah, but what are you going to do?"

"I don't know. But I do know what you're going to do."

"And what might that be?"

"You're going to tell me what's going on with Canfield Davis' secretary and then—"

"Alleged secretary," Coltraine interrupted.

"Aw, shit. You couldn't even connect him to Midwest Avionics?"

"Sorry, Nash. I agree the voice on your tape sounds a lot like Hank Spielman's, but according to our investigation, your intruder is nothing more than an out-of-work dental assistant."

"Dental assistant? Well, he tried to give me a major cavity."

"And since you taped that conversation illegally," Coltraine said evenly, "there's not much more I can do."

"You can threaten Spielman, tell him he's going down and his boss is walking away clean."

"Already tried it. Hank Spielman is just about as tough

as they come under interrogation. If Canfield Davis did hire him, he's got excellent taste in henchmen."

"I'll pass along the compliment next time I talk to him."

"Do me a favor and wait until we have a chance to question him tomorrow," Coltraine said. "There's a chance we might catch him in some kind of slip-up."

"Not with his lawyer there. They're both slicker than motor oil."

"You're probably right, but this is still an open case and I'm still in charge."

"What time does Davis jet back into town?"

"Sometime this evening, we're told."

Nash snapped his fingers. "What about the military connection? Did Spielman and Davis serve anywhere together?"

"Nope. As far as official records are concerned, Hank Spielman and Canfield Davis never crossed paths."

"Some open case."

"We do what we can, Nash."

He hung up and looked over at Povaric, who washed down several painkillers with a Coke.

"We're fucked," Nash said. "There's no way we can link Davis and Spielman over the weekend."

"Maybe not by the book," Povaric said.

"What did you have in mind?"

"You know, desperate times, desperate measures."

"How desperate?"

"Let me ask you one thing first: Is this as personal for you as it is for me?"

"Why am I staying at your place tonight?"

"Because your girlfriend's mad at you."

"That's not what I meant."

"Because you no longer have an address of your own."

"Right. I got my neighbor killed, Jerry. And I lost a little piece of my soul when I pulled the trigger on Tony Knuckles in Sam's apartment. Shit, that bastard Davis even murdered my pet squirrel."

Nash slapped the desk. "Yeah, Jerry," he said. "I think I'm about ready for a little payback."

Chapter Thirty-One

Nash called Palwaukee, the northwest suburban commuter airport, and found out Canfield Davis' jet was scheduled to land about 6 p.m. Then, after a hearty German meal at the Burghoff and quick stops at a Rush Street bondage-and-discipline shop and a Sharper Image outlet on the Magnificent Mile, Nash and Povaric headed into the 'burbs to stake out the runway.

"Maybe this isn't such a good idea," Povaric said as he passed the Wild Turkey bottle over to the driver's seat.

"What the hell, there's nothing good on TV tonight," Nash said. He pulled out the cork and took a long swig.

"What about the cops?"

"Coltraine said they weren't going to talk to Davis until tomorrow."

"Still, we could go up on kidnapping charges."

"Remind me, Jerry, who came up with this plan in the first place?"

Povaric took back the bottle, wiped the opening with his shirt sleeve, and drank. "You're right," he said, leaning back against the seat as the bourbon began to take hold. "I guess I just need a little more of this liquid courage."

At 6:09 p.m., Canfield Davis' Lear jet touched down and began coasting toward the head of the runway, where the BMW was parked. Nash looked in his rear-view mirror and saw a limousine coming their way through the parking lot gate.

"Looks like company."

Povaric kicked the empty Turkey bottle onto the gas pedal as he turned around to take a look. "I was hoping his ride would wait for him outside."

"We'll have to make this quick," Nash said. He felt a little light-headed. Luckily, the bottle had been half empty when they'd started on it. "Can you shift the stick with your arm all banged up?"

Povaric nodded. "It's only a sprain."

"Okay then." Nash climbed out of the BMW holding the softball bat against his left side, out of sight of the limo driver. As the plane approached, Povaric got out of the car and walked around to the driver's side. Two technicians wearing big orange earmuffs ran forward to coax the jet into its proper slot. The high-pitched whine of the engines made Nash wish he had some noise protection, too.

When the plane executed a half-turn and came to a stop, Nash ducked under the fuselage and waited for the steps to come down. About three minutes later, he heard metallic footsteps and saw the staircase sway under the weight of a large man. The hands on the rail were well manicured, old, strong. The cuffs of a starched white shirt lapped out of the dark blue sleeves of the man's suit just so. It had to be Canfield Davis.

As he emerged from under the fuselage, Nash saw the lower half of Davis' body moving toward the limo, about a hundred yards away. He walked directly between Nash and the BMW. Povaric gunned the engine and brought the car in front of Davis so that only his head and shoulders could be seen by the limo driver.

"Get in the car or I'll drop you where you stand," Nash said as he walked up behind Davis.

"Okay."

"And don't turn around."

By this time, the limo driver had jumped out of the vehicle and started jogging toward the jet. As Nash pushed Davis into the back seat with the bat and followed him in, Povaric placed the blue flashing light they'd bought at Sharper Image on the BMW's roof and started toward the parking lot gate.

"You think the driver bought the undercover police act?" Povaric asked as they squealed onto the road leading to the freeway.

"My driver—and my pilot—are much sharper than that," Davis said. "And unless you kill me, I will see you both arrested for this, whoever you are."

"He doesn't even know us," Povaric said, grinning at Nash in the rear-view mirror.

"I'm the guy who's going to bring you down, Mr. Davis," Nash said, poking him in the ribs with the bat by way of introduction. "What do you think about that?"

"And I'm the guy who's gonna help him," Povaric added gleefully.

"You're that reporter, Nash Hansen," Davis said, pushing aside the bat.

"Surprised to see me alive?"

"I don't have any idea what you're talking about."

"Your secretary rolled over on you today, Davis."

"What secretary?" Davis adjusted his dark striped tie and smiled. "If I did have a secretary, she wouldn't talk out of school."

"He," Nash said.

"Whatever. And if my secretary did 'roll over' on me, you hooligans wouldn't be out here doing the police's job for them, now would you?"

"I guess you're right, Canfield," Nash said. "You're probably always right."

"Where are you taking me?"

Nash shook his head. "No questions if you want to wake up with your head still attached to your neck. Shit, Jerry, take that blue light off the roof before somebody pulls us over."

Povaric swerved across two lanes of the Drive as he removed the bubble. "Sorry," he giggled.

"You two are drunk as lords," Davis said. "If you were under my command, I'd have you both busted out of the service for this type of behavior."

"If I were under your command, Davis, I'd frag the commander," Nash said. "Now shut up before I bust your jaw."

Canfield Davis snapped his eyes forward and sat silent and stiff. Nash opened a window to let in some fresh air. This was beginning to feel like the biggest blunder of his career, maybe even his life

"Where to?" Povaric asked.

"Your place, I guess."

After dropping some coins in the tollway basket, they headed south for Chicago and into the deepening gloom.

Chapter Thirty-Two

Povaric rented a small one-bedroom apartment on Des Plaines Street, part of the gentrified near West Side. The living room window overlooked the Dan Ryan Expressway a few miles south of where it stopped being the Kennedy and a few miles north of where it crossed over the Stevenson— good Democratic names all. After securing Davis to a kitchen chair with two rolls of duct tape, they sat in the living room for nearly eight hours, drinking Cokes, playing cribbage and listening to Muddy Waters discs, sobering up for the mission ahead.

Finally, at 4 a.m., they loaded Canfield Davis into the car. Although Nash had sobered up enough to consider dropping the plan, he knew the only way out of the mess they had created was to force Davis into confessing. And the only way they were going to be able to do that was to scare the living shit out of him.

"Washington and State?" Nash asked as he guided the BMW up Des Plaines.

"I believe that is the longest one," Povaric replied.

"Where are you taking me?" Davis asked. His voice had grown increasingly shrill over the past eight hours and the lower half of his face was covered with the gooey backing of the duct tape. The eyes, however, remained imperious.

Povaric began to sing. "Ba da, bop bop ba da. Bum ba da ba da ba da ba dum." He tapped out a syncopated beat on the dashboard, and soon Nash found himself joining in.

Davis swallowed hard as if attempting to fight back tears. "You two are completely insane," he said slowly, as if he had just realized the men who abducted him might decide to take his life.

"Haven't you ever heard of 'Take the A Train'?" Nash asked. "We're going to take you on a little ride."

"Look, if it's a question of money, I've got quite a lot of it," Davis said. "I promise I'll forget this ever happened."

"If you offered to bring my downstairs neighbor back to life, to rebuild my apartment and my possessions, I might consider your request," Nash said. "Can you do any of those things?"

"Of course not. Be reasonable."

"Reason has nothing to do with anything at this point."

"We are very unreasonable men," Povaric said as Nash pulled to the curb on Washington just west of State Street.

"I swear, you have the wrong man," Davis pleaded.

"Shhh," Povaric said. He picked up the aluminum softball bat by the barrel and knocked Davis out with a short, swift stroke to the back of the head. "That's better."

No place in Chicago was more deserted than the Loop at 4:00 on a Saturday morning. Actually, except for theater traffic, most of the city's central business district was damn near empty by 9:00 every night. There weren't even any muggers about, simply because they had no one to mug. As Nash and Povaric dragged Canfield Davis' unconscious body along State Street, the scuffing of his shoes on the cobblestones could easily be heard above the sounds of the few taxis cruising Michigan Avenue two blocks east.

"They don't staff these stations twenty-four hours," Povaric said. "We'll have the place to ourselves."

They pulled Davis down the two flights of stairs leading to the Washington Street Station subway platform. Another set of steps led to a tunnel connecting the station to the O'Hare-Congress line. With its shuttered newsstands, defaced billboards and benches cluttered with trash, the platform was about as uninviting as a medieval dungeon. *A fitting comparison,* Nash thought, *especially this morning.*

"Northbound or south?" Nash asked.

"I'd say north is safer," the transit reporter said. "We'll be less likely to see any riders the next couple of stops. Not many people leaving the South Side at this hour."

Nash nodded. "How long do you think we'll have once we're on board?"

Povaric squinted at the tiled wall at the end of the long platform. "Depending on how hard the conductor's leaning on the throttle, maybe forty-five seconds."

"That long?"

"Maximum."

They heard the far-off rumbling of the Red Line train coming from the south. It sounded like it was about three stops down the line.

"We'd better wake him up," Nash said.

Povaric broke out the smelling salts he'd brought from his apartment and passed them under Davis' nose. Davis jerked awake and peered at his unfamiliar surroundings, dazed.

"You ready to talk yet?" Nash asked as the roar of the train grew louder. He could see the headlight about half a mile down the track.

"I don't know anything," Davis said. He rubbed the back of his head with his left hand.

"If that's the way you want to play it," Nash said. He reached into the back pocket of his jeans and fished out the set of handcuffs he'd purchased at the Rush Street bondage shop.

"Why are you torturing me?" Davis cried as the roar of the train echoed off the tiled walls and rounded ceiling.

"We're giving you a taste of your own medicine," Nash replied.

As the train screeched in, Povaric sprinted for the lead car, the one holding the conductor. Nash headed for the back with Davis in tow. All three cars were empty of passengers.

With one quick blow from the bat, Nash broke a jagged hole in one of the small windows in the door of the car. He opened it up, cuffed Davis' right wrist and stepped onto the train. Then Nash brought the other cuff through the window, attached it to a metal pole and closed the door. He pulled out his pocket cassette player, depressed the record button and smiled.

"Help," Davis yelled, but the din of the train pulling away from the station drowned out his plea. Nash could see through the connecting doors that Povaric was doing a good job keeping the conductor occupied, probably pretending to interview him for a story.

"Here we go," Nash said as Davis began stumbling along next to the train, yanking on the handcuffs with all his strength.

"You'll rot in hell for this," Davis said.

"If you don't start talking, you'll beat me there."

The train had begun to pick up speed and Nash estimated they had about thirty seconds before Davis slammed into the wall.

"You had my apartment bombed, didn't you?" Nash said, holding the recorder up to the broken window.

"No," Davis yelled. He could barely keep up with the

train as it started to gain decent speed.

"You sent thugs into my girlfriend's apartment to kill me," Nash said.

"No."

"First you'll hit that wall, Canfield, and then this train will sever your arm at the shoulder. Think about it."

Davis ran without speaking for perhaps five seconds, but when he glanced inside the car and saw Nash holding up the key to the handcuffs, he finally broke down.

"Yes," he hollered. "Spielman sabotaged your water heater so the explosion would look like an accident. Then I sent him to your girlfriend's apartment to kill you."

It looked to be about ten seconds to impact. Nash fumbled with the key a moment, then felt the handcuff open with a well-oiled snick. A look of relief appeared on Davis' face as he pulled his arm free of the car, but his momentum carried him head-on into the cold white tiles. As the train sped on into the tunnel, Nash caught a last glimpse of Davis crumpling into a heap on the concrete floor.

Nash hit the stop button on his tape recorder, carefully removed the cassette, and kissed it. At last, salvation was at hand.

Chapter Thirty-Three

The jail cell reeked of stale bodies and desperation. At least he and Povaric were its only occupants, Nash thought as the springs of the bunk above him squealed. Canfield Davis had not only survived, he had filed a complaint against them as soon as he had crawled up the stairs to State Street and been picked up by a passing Chicago Transit Authority police unit. By 10 a.m. Saturday, Nash and Povaric had been booked, photographed and fingerprinted. Both of them were so exhausted they fell into a deep sleep as soon as they hit the cell. Now it was 3 p.m., and they were waiting for Lorenzo Nugent to bail them out.

"At least we got the story," Nash said to the bottom of the upper mattress. Povaric grunted in reply.

"I mean, we'll file the piece as soon as we get out, and by Monday Davis is in too much trouble to even worry about us anymore."

"Quit whistling past the graveyard," Povaric said. "We'll be lucky to get off with five years in Joliet."

"You're right," Lorenzo Nugent said. He stood stiffly in front of the bars, his briefcase held squarely in front of his crotch. In his white linen suit, the *Sentinel*'s attorney looked like a saint who'd made a wrong turn into hell and didn't quite know what to do about it.

"Bail should be coming through any minute," Nugent continued. "As soon as you get out, I'd like to recommend a few criminal lawyers."

"Got a full plate there, Lorenzo?" Povaric asked. He sat up and rubbed his eyes.

"This," Nugent said, gesturing toward the bleak holding cell, "this is out of my field of expertise."

"Thanks for coming through for us," Nash said. "We appreciate everything you're doing."

A guard appeared at a set of doors down the hall. Behind him came Detective Josh Coltraine, wearing his casual weekend clothes and a very somber visage.

"I guess you're sprung," Nugent said, apparently cheered that his part in the affair was about over.

"Not quite yet," Coltraine said as the guard unlocked the cell. "I want to talk to you two assholes first."

He hustled them over to Central in ten minutes flat, never saying a word. He led them to the same interrogation room Nash had visited earlier that week, only this time the atmosphere was much less cordial. Nash and Povaric gratefully accepted coffee as Coltraine began pacing the floor.

"Nash, I expressly told you to wait until we had a chance to talk to Davis. What was it, did I fail to speak English? Refresh my memory."

"I think it was Welsh," Nash said.

Coltraine slammed a fist onto the table, knocking over his coffee cup in the process. "That's over now, okay? Whatever friendship might have been happening between us, that's all over. From now on, you don't joke with me, you don't get smart with me, you don't even say my name."

"Okay," Nash said. "Detective."

"That's better. Now would either of you bozos like counsel present for this, or can we do it quick so I can go back to pretending I have some kind of life off of this god-damn force?"

"By all means," Povaric said. "I'm ready to lay my cards on the table."

"Me, too," Nash said.

They gave a complete statement of their actions from Palwaukee on, signed it and waited while Coltraine hunted up another officer to notarize it.

"So Davis confessed, eh?" Coltraine asked when he returned. "Too bad it's just one more piece of inadmissible evidence. You guys really fucked up this time. He'll put you away for years."

"Maybe not," Nash said.

"Maybe not what?" Coltraine demanded.

"Maybe not, Detective."

"What kind of fantasy have you cooked up this time, Nash? Go ahead, let loose. I need a laugh."

"We're going to run the story."

"The hell you are."

"You can't stop us, Detective. Davis' confession may not hold up in court, but it sure meets the standards of modern American journalism."

"Did you ever stop and think Davis would have admitted to being the reincarnation of Adolph Hitler if it would convince you to let him loose?" Coltraine asked.

Nash shook his head. "He knew the details. He became quite specific as that wall came closer."

"So you print the story," Coltraine said. "Then what happens? Tooth Fairy comes and bops him on the head?"

"Think about it a minute, Detective. What if we slip a copy of the early edition to Davis' 'secretary,' Hank Spielman?"

Coltraine nodded and gave Nash his first smile of the afternoon. "You get that story to me as soon as the ink dries. Let's see just how loyal our boy Spielman really is."

"I get the feeling he sees it as a two-way street."

"For your sake, I sure hope so. By the way, I hate to say this, but I'm really starting to like that Tom Jones guy. And that's strictly off the record."

"Don't worry, Coltraine," Nash said as he stood up to leave. "Your secret's safe with me."

Chapter Thirty-Four

Midwest Avionics Chief Admits Buying Weapons Plans From ex-KGB Agent, Engaging in Murder-for-Hire Plot

by Nashua Hansen and Jerry Povaric of the Sentinel

Canfield Davis, President and CEO of suburban defense contractor Midwest Avionics, Inc., has admitted violating federal arms procurement laws by purchasing plans for Russian military hardware from an ex-KGB agent. Davis also admits he moved to suppress this information by hiring two assassins to murder Sentinel *staff writer Nashua Hansen.*

Davis, who remains at large, says he ordered his personal secretary, Henry Spielman, to convert a hot water heater in Hansen's apartment into a crude but powerful bomb. The subsequent explosion demolished Hansen's Evanston apartment building June 16, killing another resident, Jake Brooks, 27.

Early on the morning of June 18, Davis says he again dispatched Spielman to kill Hansen. At about 3:15 a.m., Spielman and known hit man Tony "Knuckles" Mazzoni entered a River North apartment via the living room window. Both men were armed. In the ensuing confrontation, Hansen shot and killed Mazzoni and subdued Spielman, who is currently being held on attempted murder charges at Cook County Jail.

"Hank Spielman sabotaged the heater to make the explosion look like an accident," Davis told Hansen early Saturday morning. "Then I sent him to the apartment to kill you."

The botched cover-up was set into motion after a June 15 phone conversation in which Davis told Hansen Midwest Avionics had illegally purchased plans for Russian military airplane components from an ex-KGB agent living in Chicago.

The retired Soviet spy, Andrei Kosarov (alias Andrew Bond), was selling military secrets out of a trade show booth at the Winter National Electronics Exhibition in Atlanta in January, and at the summer exposition in Chicago earlier this month. Photographic records found in Kosarov's Lake Point Tower apartment indicate he met with members of the U.S. and foreign governments as well as Dr. Frederic Hintz, a noted animal medicine researcher at the University of Illinois-Chicago.

According to classified U.S. intelligence reports, Kosarov began his KGB career by eliminating enemies of the Soviet state in Moscow. Transferred to London in 1987, Kosarov became known in the West as The Hoarder because of his penchant for selling military and industrial secrets to the highest bidders. After the fall of the Soviet Union, Kosarov disappeared, until his body was found in a passenger shuttle at O'Hare June 10. Davis has denied any involvement in Kosarov's death, but police are still investigating the crime.

Davis launched Midwest Avionics, Inc., in 1982. During the Reagan and first Bush administration, MAI received many lucrative defense aviation contracts. In 2003, MAI held contracts worth $300 million. A career military man, Davis served on the Joint Chiefs of Staff from 1970 to 1977.

If convicted on all probable charges, Davis could be sentenced to life in prison. Spielman's trial will convene August 14.

Chapter Thirty-Five

Nash and Povaric called Coltraine down to the station at noon Sunday to have a look at their story. Nash wondered if Canfield Davis subscribed to the *Sentinel*. If so, he was probably having trouble keeping down his waffles right about now.

"You want to stick around and watch this?" Coltraine asked as he peeled off his Loyola sweat shirt.

"Might be fun," Povaric said. He ate half a breakfast burrito in one bite.

Coltraine had called ahead to have Hank Spielman brought over to homicide for questioning. They found Davis' secretary cooling his heels in an interrogation room outfitted with a one-way mirror.

"You guys wait here," Coltraine said. "These are the best seats, anyway."

They watched the detective enter and heard him exchange pleasantries with Spielman over the chamber's rudimentary sound system.

"You seen the news yet this morning?" Coltraine asked. He waved the rolled up front section enticingly in front of Spielman's nose. "Or do you maybe want to speak to your lawyer before you answer that question?"

"What are you harassing me for, detective?" Spielman asked. "I can't imagine there'd be anything in that rag worth reading."

"You never know." Coltraine unfolded the paper and smoothed it down on the table. "You never know when your name might be splashed all over the front page."

Spielman read the story with his fists clenched at his sides. When he reached the part where Davis implicated him in the apartment bombing and the murder of Jake Brooks, his cool veneer collapsed.

"Motherfucker!" Spielman barked, banging his forehead on the table repeatedly. "Motherfucking motherfucker."

"So what do you say, Spielman? You thinking about maybe changing your story now that the boss has rolled over on you?"

"Get my lawyer in here," Spielman said, his voice cracking. "And tell the DA I want to make a deal."

Coltraine gave Spielman pat on the back. "I just knew you'd find something interesting to read in here besides the funnies," he said.

Nash and Povaric were so pleased their last-minute shot had gone in the hoop that they didn't even notice the dark Taurus until it humped over the curb and blocked their path into the intersection. Just like in the movies, the back door flew open and a gun pointed out at them from inside. They climbed in without even having to be asked.

"If you're on the Canfield Davis defense team, you should know the clock just ran out," Nash said to the stranger squeezed in next to him. He hated sitting in the middle seat, especially when there was a gun sticking in his ribs.

"Wrong team," the man in the front passenger seat said as the driver merged smoothly into traffic.

Nash took in the scene. His uncomfortably close neighbor and the two men in the front seat looked like clones—close-cropped hair, white dress shirts, ties, dark blazers. They were in their indeterminate thirties, all in the pink of health.

"Feebs," Povaric confirmed.

"I'm hurt," the front-seat passenger said. "We're the good guys here. No need for insults."

"Can we see some IDs?" Nash asked. He caught the driver's half-smile in the rearview.

"Sure, we can make this an official visit, if that's what you want," the front passenger said. "We'll tell you our names, pull out our badges and then arrest you both on kidnapping charges."

"Don't forget impersonating a federal agent," the driver said.

"What?" Povaric said.

"The Lake Point Tower manager said you told him you were with us when you visited Andrew Bond's apartment," the passenger said.

"We told him we were reporters," Nash said.

"Okay, I'll take your word for it. So that just leaves the airport kidnapping of a defense contractor. Think what a jury will do with that."

"You're bluffing," Povaric said, although he didn't sound convinced.

"Maybe so," the passenger replied. "But we've got the USA Patriot Act on our side now. That kidnapping fits our guidelines for terrorist acts. We could declare you enemy combatants and make you disappear down a very dark hole for a very long time. Not even your mamas could find you, let alone your lawyers."

As Nash and Povaric exchanged a quick, sober glance, the car took an exit onto Lower Wacker Drive.

"You guys have come a long way from J. Edgar Hoover

to John Ashcroft," Nash said. "Fairies to fascists." That got a rise out of his seatmate, who used his free hand to deliver a solid love tap to his thigh. But the gun remained steadily aimed at his ribs.

"Congratulations, Nash," the front passenger said. "You're exposed yourself as both a homophobe and a conspiracy theorist."

"I'm a realist, too. What's the play?"

"We've had our eye on you for quite a while, Mr. Hansen. We were gathering evidence on those survivalist gun runners in San Bernardino when you fucked the whole thing up. And now you intrude on a delicate national security investigation involving Russian state secrets and a corrupt U.S. weapons dealer. To put it bluntly, we're sick of you shitting all over our hard work."

Nash took a deep breath. How was he going to make this problem go away?

"That reminds me of a joke," Povaric said.

"Yeah?" the talkative agent said. "I like jokes. You guys want to hear a joke?" If the other two agents nodded, Nash missed it.

"Okay," Povaric said. "One day, at a big law-enforcement convention, all the cops decide to hold a police dog contest, right? There's the local PD mutt, the sheriff's K-9 dog, the state trooper's German shepherd, and this really cocky FBI hound. So the officers set up a mock crime scene, and one by one, they send the dogs in to sniff for clues."

Povaric took in his audience: Three stone faces and a nervous reporter. He pressed on. "Well, the local PD mutt, he goes bounding through the door and comes out a few seconds later with a bloody shirt. His trainer says, 'Good job, Sparky. Attaboy.' The sheriff's K-9 is next. He races

208

in, and comes out about a minute later with a smoking gun in his mouth. 'Way to go, Ace.' No sooner does Ace come running than the state trooper's dog dives into the scene and comes out with a severed hand!

"So now everyone's watching the FBI dog. A real prize bitch. And what do you know? She runs into the house, pisses on all the evidence, then comes back outside and holds a press conference."

As Povaric finished, the car screeched off the roadway into a dark loading dock. Nash thought he saw the driver smile again.

"You've got balls, my friend," the front passenger said. "What's the point beyond the punch line?"

"Just that Nash nailed the bad guys in both those cases," Povaric snarled. "If you guys are so upset about losing out on the glory, go ahead and shoot us."

Nash almost fainted when the door locks snapped open.

"Quit making messes for us to clean up, Mr. Hansen," the front passenger said. "Get yourself a nice little features beat. Write about gardening or cookbooks or Jennifer Aniston's latest hairdo. But stay the fuck away from federal investigations. I don't even want you reviewing movies about the FBI. This is your free friendly warning. Next time, I guarantee you'll do hard time in John Gotti's old cell down in Marion. Now get the fuck out, and take Shecky here with you."

Later that evening, the phone rang in Povaric's apartment.

"You want me to get that?" Nash asked.

"Yeah," Povaric called from the kitchen. "I'm up to my armpits in garlic here."

Nash crossed his fingers and picked up the receiver. "Yes?"

"That you, Nash?"

"Yeah, Coltraine. What do you have for us?"

"Good news and bad news. Spielman made a deal with the DA's office."

"Fantastic." Nash decided not to share their little FBI adventure with the detective. In fact, he and Povaric had agreed never to speak of it again.

"I thought you'd enjoy that one," Coltraine said. "He's giving up Davis; in return, they're letting Spielman cop to manslaughter and two counts of breaking and entering. He'll do seven to ten easy."

"What's the bad news?"

"Even though Davis will probably go down on everything from illegal arms purchases to accessory to murder, the DA plans to follow through on those kidnapping and aggravated assault charges against you and Jerry."

"Shit." They had escaped the federal frying pan only to end up in the state's fire.

"I can't say that I blame him, Nash. You stepped way over the line. It doesn't matter that you did it for the right reasons. And when you combine Davis' testimony with those statements you gave to me yesterday, you're looking at doing real time on this one."

"Thanks for calling, Coltraine."

"One more thing: I'd keep the shutters closed tonight. Spielman's out on bail until sentencing next week and Canfield Davis is on his own recognizance until his prelim hearing Tuesday morning."

"The hills are alive with scumbags."

"Good luck, Nash. You piss me off, but for some reason, I kind of like you."

"All that Tom Jones music is making you soft."

"You're probably right," he chuckled.

As Nash hung up, Povaric emerged from the kitchen with two heaping plates of angel hair pasta in a light sauce of extra virgin olive oil, sage, six cloves of garlic—chopped—and freshly grated Parmesan.

"Simple, yet filling," Povaric said.

"We'd better enjoy this good cooking while we can," Nash said.

"They're sticking us with the charges?"

"Looks that way. Man, Jerry, this tastes as good as anything you'd get on Taylor Street."

"Grazie."

"You could leave town," Nash said after slurping up a mass of tender noodles. Olive oil sprayed the front of his shirt.

"What the hell are you talking about?"

"I got you into this mess, and I don't want to see you in prison because I went off the deep end."

Povaric shook his head and pointed a dripping fork at Nash. "I'm a big boy; no one twisted my arm. Besides, what are we talking about here? A guy who tried to kill you twice, blew up your neighbor, destroyed your house and left his hired help on the hook. Canfield Davis is a slug. Even if we'd killed him, I wouldn't feel the least bit guilty about it."

"I don't mind bending the rules when it's necessary," Nash said. "But this was different. This was strictly vengeance. The story became secondary." He couldn't help thinking that Reg Devonshire had been right all along.

"Why are you being so hard on yourself? Davis deserved to be knocked down three or four pegs."

"But we could have gotten the story some other way. More background research on Hank Spielman might have turned up a connection between him and Davis. We could have talked to whatever organization Tony Knuckles was affiliated with. Hell, we might have even been able to bluff our way inside Midwest Avionics for a look at their files."

"Shit, Nash, that would have taken weeks. We were working on deadline and we leaned on a dirtbag. End of story."

"Maybe so." Nash swirled the Chianti in his glass. "But I'm still sorry I got you involved."

"Don't sweat it, pal. Look at the bright side: A few years in prison will give us a chance to start writing those novels we're always talking about."

Nash held up his glass in salute. "But before we put on those orange jumpsuits and start typing, I want to track down Virgil Hoops and wrap up the Maynard Pike and Andrei Kosarov murders."

"I agree," Povaric said, clinking his glass with Nash's. "That is, if we still have the assignment."

Chapter Thirty-Six

"I should fire you both on the spot," Avery Graf said. There wasn't even a hint of a smile on his face.

"Yes," Nash replied.

"I agree," said Reg Devonshire.

Only Jerry Povaric, who pretended to scrutinize a Jackson Pollock painting on a side wall of Graf's office, declined to offer an opinion.

"What do you have to say for yourself, Jerry?" Graf asked. The publisher was clearly annoyed one of his employees would treat such a grave matter so lightly.

Povaric turned and kicked gently at a corner of the Oriental rug. "Well, Avery," he said, "so far I've seen our story picked up by CNN, *The New York Times*, the *Los Angeles Times*, the *Washington Post*, and all the networks. Unless I'm mistaken, all of the stories mentioned the *Chicago Daily Sentinel* rather prominently—and positively."

"Point well taken," Graf said.

"Still," Nash said quietly, "I realize I made a mistake. I take full responsibility and I'm not planning to let this sort of thing happen again."

"I should think not," Devonshire said. "If I had my druthers, you'd be banished from the trade for pulling a stunt like this."

"And the only reason Reg doesn't get his wish right now is because I feel I bear some responsibility for your extreme actions," Graf added. "I shouldn't have pushed you to wrap up the investigation by this morning."

Povaric took a seat next to Nash. "What's the bottom line, chief?"

Graf swiveled back and forth for a long moment, his hands pressed together in the prayer position, his index fingers touching his lips. Finally, he tapped the copies of Nash's and Povaric's depositions on the desk in front of him.

"These don't look good," he said. "Lorenzo Nugent tells me they're as good as guilty pleas. But I'm willing to stick with you both until the jury's had a chance to decide. You'll finish investigating the Maynard Pike murder, at which time you'll be suspended with pay until the end of your trial."

Graf paused and squinted hard at the managing editor. "And if you're somehow acquitted," he added, "we'll give you each a six-month severance package and wish you good luck catching on at another paper."

Devonshire's neck muscles strained so hard against his collar that Nash was surprised the top button didn't fly off his shirt and hit Graf in the forehead.

"This is outrageous," he said.

Graf shrugged. "I know where you stand, Reg, and I appreciate your position. But I want that Pike story, and then I want this situation to go away as quietly as possible. If I'm wrong, I'm prepared to face the consequences."

Devonshire shoved his arm between the closing doors of the elevator just when Nash and Povaric thought they had escaped.

"If you had any integrity at all, which I'm convinced you don't, you'd have your resignations on my desk this afternoon," the managing editor said as they descended to the newsroom level.

"Innocent until proven guilty," Povaric countered.

"Ethics," Devonshire shouted. "I'm talking about a severe breach of journalistic ethics. It makes no difference what some jury decides."

Nash took a leaf out of Josh Coltraine's handbook. "Maybe so," he said. "But what are you going to do?"

"You both may be smug and satisfied now," Devonshire replied, "but just wait and see what happens when your big protector Avery Graf accepts his position in the governor's cabinet. From what I hear, he's almost a lock for Transportation Secretary. And when that happens, you'll find my footprints all over your backs. No last story. No severance package. Only the public humiliation you deserve."

"We'll see," Povaric said.

As they walked back to their desks, Nash tapped Povaric on the shoulder. "What was that about?"

"You have to remember, Nash, you're talking to the transportation reporter here."

"And?"

"I got a call Friday morning from one of my sources in Springfield. They're going with a downstater."

"Why have you been sitting on it?"

"Enlightened self-censorship. I figured Avery would want to let me know about the selection in his own way and his own time."

Nash laughed. "So we're safe from the wrath of Devonshire."

"Until we wrap up the story, anyway." Povaric broke into a broad grin and shook his head. "You know, whoever said information is power couldn't have been more right. Now all we have to do is find Pike's killer, get ourselves acquitted and find new jobs."

"I'm sorry I got you into this, Jerry."

"Don't be. Devonshire's right. We ran across the line on this one, and I never even thought about backing out. Whatever happens to both of us, we deserve it."

Samantha called at 9:45, as they were getting ready to go beat the streets for Virgil Hoops.

"Hey," she said, "congratulations on your big scoop."

"You don't know the half of it," Nash replied.

"You sound down."

"Just determined."

"I wanted to call you last night, but I wasn't sure where you were staying."

"I've been bunking with Jerry Povaric the last couple of days."

"Tell him I said hello."

Nash put his palm over the receiver and said, "Samantha says hi."

Povaric gave him the thumbs-up.

"Are you still there, Nash?"

"Uh huh. How's tricks?"

"I'm pretty tired this morning. Haven't been sleeping much."

"Why's that?"

"Just because I kicked you out doesn't mean I don't miss you."

Nash turned his back on Povaric and lowered his voice. "I've missed you, too. As a matter of fact, I could sure go for a hug right about now."

"Can you wait until this evening?"

"I might last that long."

"I'll keep my fingers crossed. Why don't we meet somewhere?"

"Okay. What time?"

"About eight. Thai One On sound all right?"

"They don't serve booze."

"You can bring your own bottle."

"I'm going to need ice."

"Okay," she said, beginning to sound a little peeved. "Where do you want to go?"

"Why don't you let me take you to the Pump Room? It'll give me a chance to show off some of those fancy threads you bought."

"Oh, Nash, you are full of surprises."

"Then it's a date."

"Wear the blue blazer, white shirt and dark tie."

"What, no pants?"

"Tan slacks, silly. I thought you could figure that one out for yourself."

"See you soon, Sam."

"I can't wait. And Nash?"

"Yes?"

"You'll probably want to wear some shoes with that outfit, too."

Chapter Thirty-Seven

They started at the Division Street soup kitchen. No leads. They hunted in every alley and vacant lot on the near South Side, revisited the park where Povaric had been beaten, the bombed-out building Virgil Hoops had recently been calling home, even the vast network of shadowed streets underneath the Loop. Still no dice.

"It's getting dark and I'm getting tired," Povaric said. He and Nash sat in the BMW with their heads glued to the headrests, watching the rush hour traffic creep by on Michigan Avenue.

In the rearview mirror, Nash saw three mounted cops loading their rides into the back of a blue-and-white trailer. No wonder this block of East Lake Street was covered with horse shit. Just like his life.

"I've got to stop by your place and change clothes before I pick up Sam," he said. "So just say the word and we'll pack it in."

"Fuck!" Povaric shouted suddenly.

"That wasn't the word."

"Where's the last place we're going to look for Virgil Hoops?"

"Cancun?"

"Think, shithead—the place where his roommate got knifed. McCormick Place parking garage."

"If he's not already halfway to Atlanta on a boxcar

or something."

"Why would he leave the city?" Povaric asked.

"Because the cops were after him."

"Questioned and released."

"Because you were after him."

"As far as he knew I was some two-bit scumbag out to roll him. He never saw me the first day I fingered him in the soup kitchen; I just called in the cops, remember?"

"So Virgil Hoops is probably out roaming the streets without a care in the world."

"Except for where his next meal is coming from and how he's going to make it through the night without some predator slashing his throat."

"And he might feel safe again in a nice warm storeroom in a cozy little underground parking garage with a lake view right at the top of the stairs."

"It's worth a try," Povaric said. He raised his sprained arm, now wrapped in an Ace bandage. "I'm itching to hit the jackpot on this one."

Nash passed a bill through the window to the parking attendant, then eased the BMW into the nearest slot.

"Wait a second," he said as Povaric started to open the passenger door. "We need to talk."

"Don't tell me I'm waiting in the car," Povaric said. He pushed the door open a few more inches. "Because I am not waiting in the car while the man who put me in the hospital might be slumbering peacefully in a storage closet forty yards away."

"Jerry, you're waiting in the car."

"Fuck you, man."

"Look, I've been thinking about this all the way over. It's the only way. Hoops has seen you. If you come in with me, he'll bolt. And then we're back to square one."

"And if you go in alone, he'll beat the crap out of you, too. At least the two of us will have a chance to subdue him."

"And then what? Get him to spill his guts and kill him? Because if we leave him alive it's just another kidnapping charge on our ever-lengthening rap sheet. We're not thugs, Jerry. We have to start drawing a few lines. If my way means losing the story, I can live with that. But I can't live with another beating on my conscience—no matter how deserving the victim."

Povaric slowly closed the door and sank back into his seat. "Thank you, Jiminy Cricket," he said. He sounded pissed, but Nash could tell that was only because he hated to be wrong.

Nash climbed out and leaned back inside the door. "Thanks, buddy," he said. "If I'm not back in ten minutes, forget everything I just said."

"With pleasure."

Thick concrete walls separated each level of the two-story structure into eight smaller parking areas. A pedestrian walkway ran along one end of each wall; at the other, a driveway allowed cars to pass between sections. During an auto show or other popular public event, this set-up allowed for maximum efficiency in moving customers in and out. When each section filled up, garage attendants placed sawhorse barricades in the middle of the lane and started guiding cars into the remaining open areas.

Today, however, with McCormick Place lying empty as the ruins of a Greek amphitheater, the layout of the garage served only to give Virgil Hoops more corners out of which to spring and surprise someone. Nash crept slowly from pillar to pillar, starting at every echo caused by dripping pipes or far-off footsteps. When he finally reached the storage room where he had seen Maynard Pike lying in a pool of his own blood what seemed like months ago, he only had about five minutes left before Povaric would come charging to the rescue. He knocked gently on the door.

No sound came from the storage room. Nash put an ear to the door, but he only heard the sound of his own breathing.

"Hello in there," he called out pleasantly, stepping three feet back.

Still no sound.

Nash scratched the back of his neck with his left hand and found the fine hairs there standing straight up. Even his body sensed this was the make-or-break moment. As confidently as he could, he walked up to the heavy metal door, twisted hard on the knob and yanked it open. Artificial light flooded into the dark quarters as a nearly intolerable stench flooded out. Standing there with his hand over his nose and mouth, Nash thought for a second that he'd come too late, that someone else, someone lethal, had gotten to Virgil Hoops first. But then the figure cowering in the corner of the room raised its head and spoke.

"Whatever it is, I didn't do it," Virgil Hoops said. His eyes danced with an almost inhuman fear, and Nash could see Hoops was on the verge of striking out at the perceived threat he represented.

Nash held out his hands, palms up, and smiled weakly. "They're empty," he said. "I'm not here to hurt you."

Hoops grunted an unbelieving grunt and moved onto his haunches, ready to spring forward.

"I'm here from the newspaper, the *Daily Sentinel*," Nash said. "I'm going to reach into my shirt pocket now and pull out some identification."

He fished out his press badge and a ten-dollar bill and tossed them toward Hoops. Although the man's eyes followed the arc of the throw, his fists remained clenched and he made no move to pick up either the ID or the money resting at his feet.

"Don't need no subscription," Hoops said.

"That's good, because we don't deliver to parking lots."

"Go away."

"Can't leave without my ID."

Hoops bent over, grabbed the card off the floor and flung it out of the room without looking at it.

"I want to talk to you," Nash said. "I'll pay you well for just a little of your time. I'll get you a good hot meal. I'll get you some help."

"Don't need any help," Hoops snarled.

"Is that what you're after?" Nash asked. "Freedom? No one bugging you?"

Hoops seemed to soften at the mention of the word. Although he stayed on his haunches, ready to fight, he cocked his head slightly, as if willing to listen.

"That's it, right?" Nash continued. "Don't fence me in."

"Yeah," Hoops whispered.

"I respect that, believe me. I want you to enjoy your freedom even more than you do now. Would you like that?"

"Maybe." He stood up now, placing his hands on his knees as he began to feel the stretch in his calf muscles from crouching so long.

"Here's the deal," Nash said. "I need to talk to a freedom lover like you for a story I'm working on. You answer my questions for a few hours this evening and I'll give you another fifty bucks to go with that ten."

Hoops laughed sharply. "Nothing's that easy."

"Oh, I agree," Nash said, leaning over to pick up his

press badge. "I'm not saying some of my questions won't be difficult. But if you tell me what I need to know, you just walk away. I'll never bother you again."

Hoops took a step forward and Nash fought the urge to back off.

"Let me see that thing," Hoops said, pointing at the badge.

"Do we have a deal?" Nash asked when the man had scrutinized the ID and handed it back.

Hoops nodded solemnly and leaned over to pick up the bill. "I walk out whenever I want."

"Agreed. But you only get the money if you answer all my questions."

Hoops paused then and Nash could see he was having second thoughts, so he pulled out his wallet and extracted two twenties and a ten.

"You could enjoy an awful lot of freedom with this, I imagine."

Hoops made a grab for the money but Nash stepped back quickly enough to send the man stumbling past him like a confused bull.

"You roll me and I'll have the cops all over you by midnight," Nash said. "Not much freedom in that."

It only took Hoops a second to think it through. "Let's talk," he said.

Chapter Thirty-Eight

Nash hoped Virgil Hoops wouldn't remember what Jerry Povaric looked like, but as soon as they got close enough to see inside the windshield of the 2002, Hoops jumped back and exclaimed, "I'm not riding with that piece of shit."

Nash tried to calm him down, offering Hoops an extra twenty. He cast a sharp glance at Povaric to keep him from getting out and exacting revenge for last week's beating.

"It don't matter how much money you give me," Hoops said after a few minutes of intense lobbying from Nash. "There's no way in hell I'm getting in a car with that man. He damned near killed me in the park a few days ago."

Povaric laughed and held up his bandaged arm. "Bullshit," he said. "Your memory's gone south on you, old man."

"I don't care what he says, that man was after me last week," Hoops said.

"He's a reporter like me," Nash said. "He only wanted to talk."

Hoops scowled. "Whatever kind of set-up this is, you can count me out."

"Wait one second," Nash said. He turned to Povaric and gave him his best plaintive smile. "It looks like you're a deal breaker here, Jerry."

"What are you talking about?"

"You heard the man. He's afraid of you."

"*He's* afraid of me? And what do you want me to do about that, huh? Tell him pretty please with sugar on top?"

"Not exactly. I want you to catch a taxi home."

Povaric shook his head firmly. "No way, Nash. There's just no fucking way."

"You can't tell me you want to lose the story over something stupid like this, after all the shit we've been through."

"I said no."

"I'll make it up to you, I promise. How about season tickets to the Bears?"

The offer caught Povaric off-guard. "Really?" he asked, grinning like a kid at his first peep-show.

"If they're available."

"Don't worry, Nash, I'll find some."

"Okay then. But I'll need your keys, too."

"First you make me find a cab at six o'clock in front of an empty convention center; now you want to take this shitheel to my apartment?"

"The keys, Jerry. It's the only way."

When they'd gotten Hoops situated in the front seat and rolled all of the BMW's windows down for maximum ventilation, Nash clapped Povaric on the back and climbed in.

"By the way, I'm going to need to lend Virgil one of your sweat suits," Nash said as he backed out of the space. "I'm afraid my clothes will be too small on him."

He accelerated up the ramp, so fast he couldn't quite make out Povaric's response. But if the heavy clang of his partner's fist on the trunk lid was any indication, Nash was sure the language had been colorful.

Nash barely survived the drive over, even with a stiff wind blowing off the lake. *Hoops could market his body odor as a chemical weapon,* he thought as he led the big, bedraggled transient up to Povaric's apartment. It was 6:45;

Samantha would soon arrive at the Pump Room for their let's-get-reacquainted dinner.

"Do you have anything against showers?" Nash asked as he cranked open the big living-room window.

"That your idea of a smart remark?" Hoops asked, making himself at home on the futon couch.

"Nope. Just wondering."

"I guess you can tell I haven't had one in quite a while."

"Uh huh."

"It's more from lack of opportunity than anything else."

"You're in luck then," Nash said. "There's a full-service bathroom right at the end of the hallway. You'll find clean towels in the linen closet on the left."

"I don't really feel like a shower."

"I've got an extra twenty bucks that says you do."

"What're we up to now, a hundred?"

"Eighty, but who's counting."

"All right, I'll run myself under the tap."

"Why not try standing under it a while? I'll lay some clean clothes out in front of the door for when you're finished."

"Do I have to use that cream rinse shit?"

"Only if you want to give your hair that extra bounce."

Nash threw on his dinner outfit and grabbed a pair of gray sweats for Hoops from Povaric's dresser. *This is going to be the most expensive interview of my life,* he thought as he knotted his tie.

"I used that blue toothbrush in there," Hoops said when he emerged from the steamy confines of the bathroom. "Hope you don't mind."

Nash laughed. "Not at all. Mine's the red one. Hey, you're not toxic anymore."

"I feel better, too. Human."

Hoops was an almost handsome man, when he didn't smile. His broken yellow teeth ruined the effect, but when he kept his mouth shut, his rugged facial features, scraggly hair and bushy black beard made Nash think of a frontier lumberjack. Even in the baggy sweats, Hoops cut an imposing figure, topping out at about six-two and weighing in at close to two-twenty-five. It wasn't difficult to see how this man had put Povaric out of commission with a few blows from those barbells he called fists.

"How come you don't clean yourself up at a shelter every now and then?" Nash asked.

"I can't stand showering with a bunch of guys staring at my joint. I'd rather stink."

"Fair enough. By the way, you might want to run a comb through your hair before we go; we're having dinner at a pretty fancy place."

Chapter Thirty-Nine

After disposing of Hoops' fetid clothes, he and Nash were on their way to the Ambassador East Hotel by 7:45. With any luck in traffic, Nash thought as he headed downtown, they'd be right on time.

To their credit, the maitre'd and the hostess who led them to their table did not make any disparaging remarks about the appearance or dress of Virgil Hoops. They simply outfitted him with a jacket and tie kept in the cloak room for just such occasions and then treated him with the same degree of deference they afforded every other customer. The fact that the Pump Room was located in the Ambassador Hotel might have had something to do with their attitude. They had undoubtedly seen more than their share of underdressed guests traipse down to the lobby for a quick meal over the years.

Within a few seconds after they'd ordered drinks—Nash had asked for his customary Wild Turkey and Hoops had requested a beer—Samantha waved at them from the top of the steps leading to the sunken dining room. To her left, half a dozen well-bred patrons tinkled glasses in the spacious piano bar while the evening's entertainment launched into a subdued version of "You're the Top."

"I didn't realize you would be bringing a guest," Samantha said, raising an eyebrow at Nash as the hostess pulled out a chair for her. "What a pleasant surprise."

"You look gorgeous," Nash said. Although he meant the comment to smooth her ruffled feathers, Sam really had gone whole hog in the glamour department. She wore a slinky, off-the-shoulder cocktail dress of shimmering black silk, a large string of pearls, diamond earrings and black stiletto pumps. Her pinned-up dark hair revealed the pale pink skin of her neck. But the most surprising aspect of her appearance was that she wore full makeup, and wore it well. It was the first time he'd seen her completely done up. He enjoyed the effect so much he failed to introduce her to Hoops for several seconds, creating an awkward silence at the table.

"I'm sorry," Nash said when he finally picked up the vibe. "Samantha Parker, this is Virgil Hoops. I'm interviewing him for a feature."

"Pleased to meet you," Sam said, extending her right hand to the stranger at her left.

"Same here," Hoops said. He took her hand, bent forward, and bestowed a damp kiss on her third knuckle.

"Oh," Samantha said. She surreptitiously wiped the back of her hand on the edge of the tablecloth.

"I'll explain everything later," Nash whispered in her ear. "I promise."

She gave him a look that screamed, *You'd better.*

"So, Virgil, you see anything you like?" Nash asked.

"I sure do."

"I was talking about the menu."

"Sorry," Hoops said, but his eyes lingered on Samantha's plunging neckline.

"The quail and pheasant here are both excellent, if you like game," Nash said. He poked Hoops in the shin with his shoe.

"Whatever." Hoops took a sip of his beer. "You gonna

play footsie with me all night, or are we going to talk some?"

Nash pulled the recorder out of his inside jacket pocket and placed it in front of Hoops' salad plate. "So, where were you born and how old are you?"

"Milwaukee, and I'm forty-three."

"What's the story about, Nash?" Samantha asked.

"The city's homeless community."

Her eyes flashed; she'd apparently made the connection with Maynard Pike's murder.

"Now where were we?" Nash asked, turning his attention to Hoops once again.

"My life story."

"Right. Why don't you just hit the high points for me."

Virgil Hoops, as one might have imagined, hadn't had a lot of high points, so the story didn't last much longer than the appetizer course. After flunking out of a Catholic high school in suburban Milwaukee, Hoops had been shipped off to some half-assed reform school in Detroit. Unfortunately, the program turned out to be little more than a recruitment center for one of the local drug lords. By eighteen, Hoops had risen to the rank of lieutenant in the organization.

As the money got better and the drugs sucked him in, he lost touch with his family. By the mid 1980s, Hoops had wormed his way into a Cincinnati heroin franchise. By 1992, he'd become so hooked on his own junk he'd lost the store. Except for a brief stint in rehab, he'd been out on the streets ever since. He was at a Chicago train station the day he decided to abort a return trip to Wisconsin in '99 and he never quite got around to leaving town.

"There wasn't anybody in Milwaukee that wanted to see me, and there wasn't really anybody there I wanted to see," Hoops said between bites of heavily buttered asparagus.

"Except I wouldn't have minded finding some of those nuns that booted me out of school to give 'em a swift kick in their habits."

When they got to the dessert course—chocolate torte all around—Nash popped a fresh tape in the recorder and leaned back in his chair.

"You enjoying yourself so far?" he asked.

"The food's fine and I sure don't mind the company," Hoops said. He gave Samantha a grotesque parody of a sly wink. "I almost feel bad getting paid for it."

"Don't," Nash said. "Because here comes the hard part. Do you have any idea why I came looking for you?"

"You wanted a close-up look at life on the streets."

"It's more than that, though. How do you think I knew your name?"

"I told it to you."

Nash shook his head, and Hoops began to fidget with his tie, a wide green number that looked like it had been left there by Al Capone.

"Don't worry, I'm not setting you up. But I do want to talk about your old partner, Maynard Pike."

Hoops gulped and swallowed too much unchewed eclair for his throat to handle. When he began choking, Samantha held a napkin under his chin. Hoops coughed up the cake and asked for a drink of water.

"I never heard of him," he said when he'd regained most of his composure.

"You sure have a funny way of reacting to names you never heard before," Nash said. "Now come on, I know the police took you in for questioning."

"They had to let me go," Hoops blurted. "They knew I didn't do it."

"At least they didn't have any proof."

"Nash, that's not a very nice thing to say," Sam interrupted. "After all Mr. Hoops has been through."

"Murder isn't a very nice business," Nash said. "But you're right, I don't think Virgil murdered his pal. However, I do believe he knows more about the killing than he told the cops."

"I didn't tell them anything," Hoops said.

"Exactly. But you're going to tell me, aren't you? Starting from where you two met."

Hoops looked over at Samantha, who smiled encouragingly.

"I saved Maynard from these crackheads in Uptown a few months ago," he began. "They were rousting him for whatever he had. When they found out he didn't have shit, they got so pissed off they started beating on his head with a pipe—and not a crack pipe, neither. I was taking a nap behind some garbage cans when I heard them yelling. I threw a couple of lids and scared 'em off. I was just trying to get some peace and quiet, but Pike treated me like I was some kind of hero."

"And then you became a team."

"More or less. I'm a pretty smart guy, you know, and strong. I do all right for myself. But you can't watch your own back twenty-four-seven. And Pike, he was good at scrounging up a meal or finding us a warm place to sleep—like that room in the parking garage. That was his idea."

"So, one fine day a couple weeks ago, you and Maynard are sleeping, eating, shooting the shit—whatever—when somebody walks by and plants a knife in your buddy's chest."

"Yeah."

"I need the specifics, Virgil."

"We're getting ready to head over to Division Street for

supper, and Maynard looks out and sees this guy coming towards us, okay? It's the end of the day, there's no one else in the garage and this guy in a suit is coming our way."

"And one of you decides to mug him."

"Hell no. I may have been a drug dealer, but I was never a thief. Neither was Maynard."

"Nah, from what I read, he just had a taste for hot cars and little girls."

"You believe what you want, friend, but I'm being straight with you. Maynard just thought this guy might be good for some loose change. So when he walks by, Pike steps out . . . And then it was like wham!" Hoops snapped his fingers and shook his head. "It all happened so goddamn quick."

"What happened?"

"The guy in the suit pulls a fucking pig sticker right out of the top of his briefcase—some kind of secret compartment—and carves Maynard up like a goddamn Christmas goose."

"Oh my God," Samantha said. "Did the man say anything?"

"Not a damn thing. He just sort of shudders for a minute—like he's really enjoying himself, you know?—then he wipes off the knife on Pike's shirt, slips it back in the briefcase and walks off like nothing happened."

"It's a miracle he didn't see you," Samantha said.

"I know. That's why I didn't say anything to the cops. I didn't want that guy hunting me down."

"He's dead," Nash said.

"Who is?"

"Andrei Kosarov, the man who killed your buddy."

"You're kidding."

"Nope."

233

"Who got him?"

Nash paused, took a sip of his third Wild Turkey, savored the burn.

"You did, Virgil," he said.

Hoops let out a nervous titter, a high-pitched sound that seemed inappropriate coming from the mouth of such a big man. "Is this some kind of joke?" he asked.

"No joke. Look, I know you killed him. Two witnesses said they saw a homeless man leave the scene."

"Hell, a lot of us bums hang out at the airport."

Nash reached out and pulled Hoops forward by his tie. "I never mentioned anything about an airport."

"Sure you did," he gasped. "Play back the tape. I know you did."

Samantha shook her head. "No he didn't, Virgil." She placed a well-manicured hand on his heaving shoulder as Nash let go of the tie. "Don't you think it's time to talk about it?"

Hoops sighed. "Yeah, okay. You got me. I killed him."

He shrugged Samantha's hand off his shoulder and looked her square in the eye. "I stabbed that fucker with his very own knife right in the middle of the airport. And then I walked away clean. Those witnesses, none of them tried to stop me. I'm surprised they even remembered seeing me. They're so used to ignoring us, we're like ghosts to them. They can't imagine we could actually do something besides beg for quarters. I bet none of them remembered a thing about me."

"You're right about that," Nash said. "In some ways, it was the perfect disguise."

"How about that? Those invisible ninjas don't have shit on us homeless guys. They ought to draft us into the fucking CIA."

"The one thing I don't understand is how you tracked Kosarov down," Nash said.

"Easy. I hot-wired an old Buick near the storage room and then I followed the bastard to his fancy apartment. After that, it was just a matter of time. I sat there all night, watching for him. When he tried to run the next morning, I followed him to the bank and then to O'Hare. You should have seen the look on his face when I walked up and pulled that knife out of his briefcase. I don't even think he understood why I was doing it, but I didn't give a shit. Just watching him die was plenty good enough for me."

"I think I'm going to be sick," Samantha said. She got up and walked briskly toward the bathroom.

"Whew," Nash said. "That is one hell of a tale."

"Yep, and it's all yours—for a hundred bucks."

Nash counted out five twenties and Hoops stuffed them into the zippered pocket of the sweatshirt.

"And now, I think I'll be on my way." Hoops stood up and dropped his napkin on the table.

"You know I have to turn you in," Nash said.

"Yeah, I know. But by the time you tell the cops what happened, I'll already have faded back into the woodwork somewhere down the line."

"Good luck, Virgil."

"Same to you, Nash. Thanks for the shower."

"Maybe it'll give you a taste for civilized living."

"I doubt if even your fine lady could do that for me."

At the top of the steps, Virgil Hoops turned and gave Nash a two-fingered salute. Nash couldn't help but return the gesture.

Chapter Forty

The U.S. District Court for Northern Illinois occupied a stately Federal Building in the south Loop, a lesser light in Chicago's pantheon of great architecture, but a light nonetheless. Fronted with massive limestone columns and pinnacled with gray dome and spire, the courthouse opened into yawning hallways adorned with New Deal murals of the Italian atom splitter Fermi, the Croatian electricity theorist Tesla and other famous immigrant inventors who'd made their reps in the Windy City. At 8:30 Tuesday morning, Nash and Povaric met on the building's wide front steps and followed a small crowd of reporters, trial junkies and less-than-innocent bystanders to the courtroom where Canfield Davis would soon be arraigned on a variety of federal charges, all of them serious felonies.

The immense room made Canfield Davis, President and CEO of Midwest Avionics, Inc., look even smaller than he really was. He tried to fill the hall with stolid self-confidence and steely determination, projecting his will to the center of the arched stone ceiling, back to the Art Deco frescoes flanking the great oak bench and over to the raised box where twelve jurors would soon decide his fate under the watchful gaze of an Abraham Lincoln bust.

Davis was attempting to back down the entire U.S. justice system with his dark, piercing eyes. But the thin trickles of sweat that ran from his forehead past his close-cropped gray sideburns and down to the damp ring of his collar gave the lie to his charade. For the first time in his life, Canfield Davis was beaten; what's worse, he realized it. Even so, he refused to drop his field general's air until the magistrates led him away in chains to some comfortable but humiliating country club prison where he would be no better, and possibly even a little bit worse, than the embezzler or the tax cheat in the bunk next to his.

No matter how the trial turned out, this was a satisfying moment for Nash. From his seat on the left side of the gallery, he could see the phalanx of lawyers Davis had stocked at the defense table. Behind them, other grim-faced defendants waited for their turn at bat and several members of the Brooks family sat ready to see the man who'd killed their Jake get his just rewards.

And there in the far corner, next to a seven-foot statue of Blind Justice, sat Hank Spielman. He wore dark glasses and a slouch, and although his sentencing wasn't scheduled until later that week, Nash guessed he had shown up to watch his handiwork come to fruition.

"I can't believe you forgot to tell me Hoops used my toothbrush," Povaric said. "I'm probably going to die of some weird fungus."

"I meant to call you, really," Nash said, trying not to laugh. "It was a busy night."

"I noticed you didn't make it back to the apartment."

"Samantha and I had a lot to talk about."

Povaric flexed his eyebrows and said, "I bet."

"And I wish. But as unbelievable as it sounds, we only talked."

"How did she take the news that her boyfriend is a felon?"

"Not well. There was a lot of crying."

"Did she come around?"

"It's hard to tell. I think my soft touch with Virgil Hoops scored me some points."

"Sorry I missed it."

"Me, too. Did you get home okay?"

"Other than the part where three guys tried to sell me crack on Twenty-third Street before I could hail a cab, I'd say the trip turned out pretty well."

"I owe you big time, Jerry."

"I want to sit close enough to the field to see the QB's five o'clock shadow."

"You've got it. Mind if I pick up a pair of tickets?"

"Might as well. It's no fun going to the games alone."

The sergeant-at-arms emerged from a side room and called the court into session. The judge, an old man with a faded black robe and rimless bifocals, looked like he hadn't had a bowel movement in about fifty years.

"I hope we don't get that guy," Povaric whispered.

"No chance. We're being tried at the state level."

The judge cleared his throat, a long dry rattle, and got the ball rolling. He'd been on the job so long he knew what the lawyers were going to say well before they did. Within five minutes, he'd set bond—a million bucks—and another preliminary hearing for Davis a few weeks down the road. The Brooks family appeared disappointed by the procedure, but Hank Spielman's expression remained impassive.

As the magistrate cuffed Davis and led him toward the main door, Nash watched Spielman rise and move along the back wall, plotting an intersecting course. Before anyone else realized what was going on, Spielman slipped between two lawyers and yanked the magistrate's sidearm out of his holster.

One of the lawyers shouted, "Gun!" But it was too late

for Davis. As the rest of the litigators dropped to the floor, the magistrate jerked wildly on the handcuffs linking him to Davis, trying to get out of the firing line. He needn't have worried; Spielman was a pro.

Three sharp reports filled the courtroom, and then it was done. Canfield Davis toppled over, pulling the untouched magistrate down with him. Where once there were a pair of steely eyes and a jutting jaw, there was now a mass of blood and brains.

And then Spielman began moving forward, over splayed legs and upturned benches. It took Nash a moment to understand he was now the target. He glanced past the Honest Abe bust to the closing door to the judge's chambers, where His Honor and the court reporter had fled. There was no way he would make it to the main courtroom door, either. Crouched down behind the far end of the bench he'd been sitting on, Nash watched the gun coming toward him, ready to make a mad leap for safety as soon as the finger tightened on the trigger.

But before Spielman could close the deal, the sergeant-at-arms drilled him in the back with two slugs from his service revolver. Betraying no emotion from behind his sunglasses, Davis' ex-secretary simply crumpled onto his knees, his gun skidding out ahead of him.

Then the sergeant's revolver went off twice more and Hank Spielman fell face first onto the marble. His wayward gun came to rest not six feet away from Nash, its barrel pointing right at him.

"Whoa," Povaric whispered. "I'll write this one up while you work on the Hoops piece."

Nash nodded, took one last look at the carnage and thought, *Couldn't have happened to two nicer guys.*

Chapter Forty-One

Before returning to the *Sentinel*, Nash and Povaric met with a slick defense lawyer in an even slicker suite of offices halfway up the Sears Tower. They gave her a blow-by-blow account of their session in the interrogation room and then told her what had transpired—and who had expired—in court that morning. When they finished, the lawyer smiled and said it might be the easiest case she'd ever had.

"She'll probably still charge us the full fee," Povaric said on the way out.

By 4:30, Povaric had finished the account of the double murder in the courtroom and Nash was putting the final touches on the Hoops story, slanting it to give Avery Graf's humanization-of-the-homeless angle maximum play.

At five, while they waited for Reg Devonshire and city editor Phil Silvestri to give the pieces their stamp of approval, Nash's phone rang.

"Why'd you have to go and tell on me?" Detective Coltraine barked.

"What the hell are you talking about?" Nash asked.

"Your lawyer just got me into a bunch of hot water with the department and the district attorney's office."

"Why? Did you forget to read us our rights or something?"

"Close. It seems I had your statements notarized after you signed them. And since the notary never actually saw you put pen to paper, the whole damn thing's invalid. Jeez, what's the world coming to when you can call a guy in on a Saturday morning and expect him to remember every procedure in the book?"

"What does that mean in terms of our case?"

"When the DA found out he'd lost both his confession and his complainant in the space of a few hours, he cussed himself a blue streak—and then he dropped all charges. You and Povaric are extremely lucky men."

"Son of a bitch!" Nash yelled. "Jerry, we're off the hook."

"I told you that lawyer was a great woman," Povaric said, grinning.

"Thanks for the news, Coltraine," Nash said.

"You don't have to sound so happy about it."

"Cheer up, buddy. I solved two more murders for you last night." He filled the detective in on his conversation with Virgil Hoops. "Of course, he was too big for me to hold," Nash added. "But I'll have a copy of the tape on your desk tomorrow morning."

A sigh came over the line. "Do me a favor and don't do me any more favors," Coltraine said.

The icing on the already wonderful day was the pained look on Reg Devonshire's face when he had to tell Nash and Povaric that both of the stories were excellent and that both would be running on page one—above the fold.

"This is the way it was meant to be done," he mumbled.

"What's that?" Silvestri asked, giving Nash a slight nudge in the ribs. "I couldn't quite make it out."

"Hey Reg, too bad about the governor stiffing Avery Graf on that cabinet appointment, huh?" Povaric said.

Devonshire's lips were pursed together so tightly they

looked like they might rupture. "Excuse me?"

"Oh, I'm sorry," Povaric said. "I guess news travels slower around here than I thought."

"Don't worry, Reg," Nash said. "You're still a relatively young man."

"Keep laughing." He handed both of them an envelope. "Here's your severance checks, as agreed. If you're not out of the building in five minutes, you'll have a security escort."

Chapter Forty-Two

Jerry was passed out across a table in the back room of Billy Goat's Tavern when Nash stumbled into the darkness at midnight. He collapsed onto a stack of pallets at the edge of a driveway down the block, pulled out his cell and dialed Samantha's number.

"It's your favorite freelancer calling," he said.

"Wow, do you sound drunk." Samantha yawned. "I was trying to get some sleep."

"Sorry. Sorry." He couldn't think of anything else to say.

"Where are you staying?"

The question hurt him. "Don't know," he mumbled.

There was a long pause. "Listen," Samantha said, "I'd invite you to stay here, but things have been so uncertain between us."

When he didn't reply, she continued. "I do miss you, Nash, really. And I know I've been going back and forth with you, but it's just all so crazy. You brought death into my house. You kidnapped a man and cuffed him to a train. You took me out on a date with a homeless man."

Nash nodded at everything she said, tears rolling down his face.

"Are you still there?" she asked.

"Yeah." He could barely get it out. He was going to be sick.

"I guess what I'm trying to say is, I think this might be

too much for me. I care about you, but things have been so out of control . . ."

"Okay," Nash said, louder than he wanted to. "I get it. Right."

"I'm sorry. Don't drive anywhere tonight, all right?"

"All right."

"Maybe in a few weeks, we can get together for lunch or something and see where we're at."

Nash shook his head, but then realized she couldn't see him. He took a deep breath.

"Sam?"

"Yeah?"

"What's your middle name?"

"What?"

"Your middle name. What is it?"

She laughed. "It's always a surprise with you, isn't it, Nash? My middle name is Eve."

"Samantha Eve Parker," he said.

"Yes."

"Goodbye, Samantha Eve Parker."

"Goodbye, Nash."

Chapter Forty-Three

In his dream, Nash and Samantha were married on one of those gorgeous late May days that make living in northern Illinois worthwhile. Samantha's three sisters served as bridesmaids, which made her little brother jealous. Standing up with Nash were Jerry Povaric, Slant Williams and Curt Escobar, his old friend from the San Bernardino *Ledger*.

The forest preserve clearing seemed almost full to bursting with life. Both their families were in attendance, along with a fair sprinkling of friends from the animal clinic and the *Daily Sentinel*. Elizabeth wasn't there, of course, but she'd phoned Nash at work to wish him well after the announcement ran. His neighbor Jake showed up a few minutes late, Cyd chittering away on his shoulder. Nash knew he ought to be irritated by the interruption, but for some reason their appearance filled him with joy.

In fact, aside from his father setting up his bulky old camcorder right in front of the seating area, getting hitched to Sam went off without a hitch. The biggest surprise came during the reception, when both sets of parents announced their decision to give the newlyweds a down payment on the house of their choice—as long as they picked one near Chicago. His mother and father even talked about moving back from Florida to be closer to their only son, and maybe a grandchild or two.

Later, they all ate dinner at the Red Apple, which Nash had rented out for the celebration. Their friend Kamil led the rest of the waitstaff in a Polish toast to wedded bliss, and everyone consumed enough champagne and iced Stoli to raise Lake Michigan an inch.

They sat at the head table with their parents, along with the groomsmen, the bridesmaids and their respective spouses and significant others. Nash couldn't get over how stunning Samantha looked in her mother's shimmering white gown. Sometimes the old styles were the best.

"Thanks for inviting us to this shindig, Rambler," Escobar said as he dug into his second plate of kielbasa. "Faye and I were a little long in the tooth for this type of production number, so we just eloped to Reno one weekend. Otherwise, I would have asked you to stand up for me, too."

Nash smiled, remembering how Escobar had married Faye Krashenko, the *Ledger*'s features editor, about a year after he'd brought them together in a San Bernardino hospital room.

"We'll make sure to invite you if we ever decide to renew our vows," Faye said. She leaned in close to him. "You'd better stop getting into so much trouble on these investigations if you want to keep her happy, Nash."

"Quit scaring the poor kid," Escobar said.

Nash lost track of the conversation when Samantha turned away from her parents and gave him a kiss that tasted like champagne.

"Oh, Nash," she whispered. "You could never drive me away."

Epilogue

Nash awoke two hours later, when a truck carrying the *Sentinel*'s bulldog edition came rumbling by his spot among the pallets.

He didn't know if he was sober enough to drive yet, didn't know what had happened to Jerry and didn't really care about any of it. He fished his keys out of his right pants pocket and walked toward the paper, where he'd parked what seemed like a year ago.

Looking up at the darkened *Sentinel* building as he started the BMW, Nash reflected on recent events. He'd lost his job, his apartment and now his girlfriend. All he had left was this rusty old car. *It's official,* he thought, *I'm living out the lyrics to a country-western song.*

He shifted into drive and hit the gas. The car lurched forward, then stopped with a clunk. Nash rolled down his window and looked out at the front driver's side wheel. Booted.

Ahead, across the Chicago River, an Orange Line train made its noisy way along the elevated tracks that encircled the Loop. Nash locked up the BMW and started off for the station.

Twenty minutes later, as the sun shot its first fiery fingers across the lake and into the windows of the city's skyscrapers, Nash was on the el to Midway Airport, resting his head against a smudged window. The only other person in his car, a young woman in full business armor, tried not to make eye contact. But he couldn't help noticing that she was reading his last page-one story in the *Chicago Daily Sentinel*. If she only knew.

As promised, the paper's severance package was generous. Big enough to give him time to put his life back together, he hoped.

From here on out, Nash vowed, he'd stop bending the rules of journalism whenever it suited him. If it cost him a big story every once in a while, so be it. It was time to grow up and build a career he could be proud of. He'd work his way back up to the top from whatever small-town daily would take him on.

But first, Nash thought as the train pulled up to the Midway platform, it was time for a vacation. He'd never been to Grand Cayman, but it was in the Caribbean and *Sports Illustrated* was shooting its swimsuit edition there, so how bad could it be?

He wondered if Elizabeth would be happy to see him.

5+/ε